Anna

and the

Flower Girl

*A Fanciful French Twist on
A Little Princess*

Amy Devins

Josy's Little Library

www.josyslittlelibrary.com

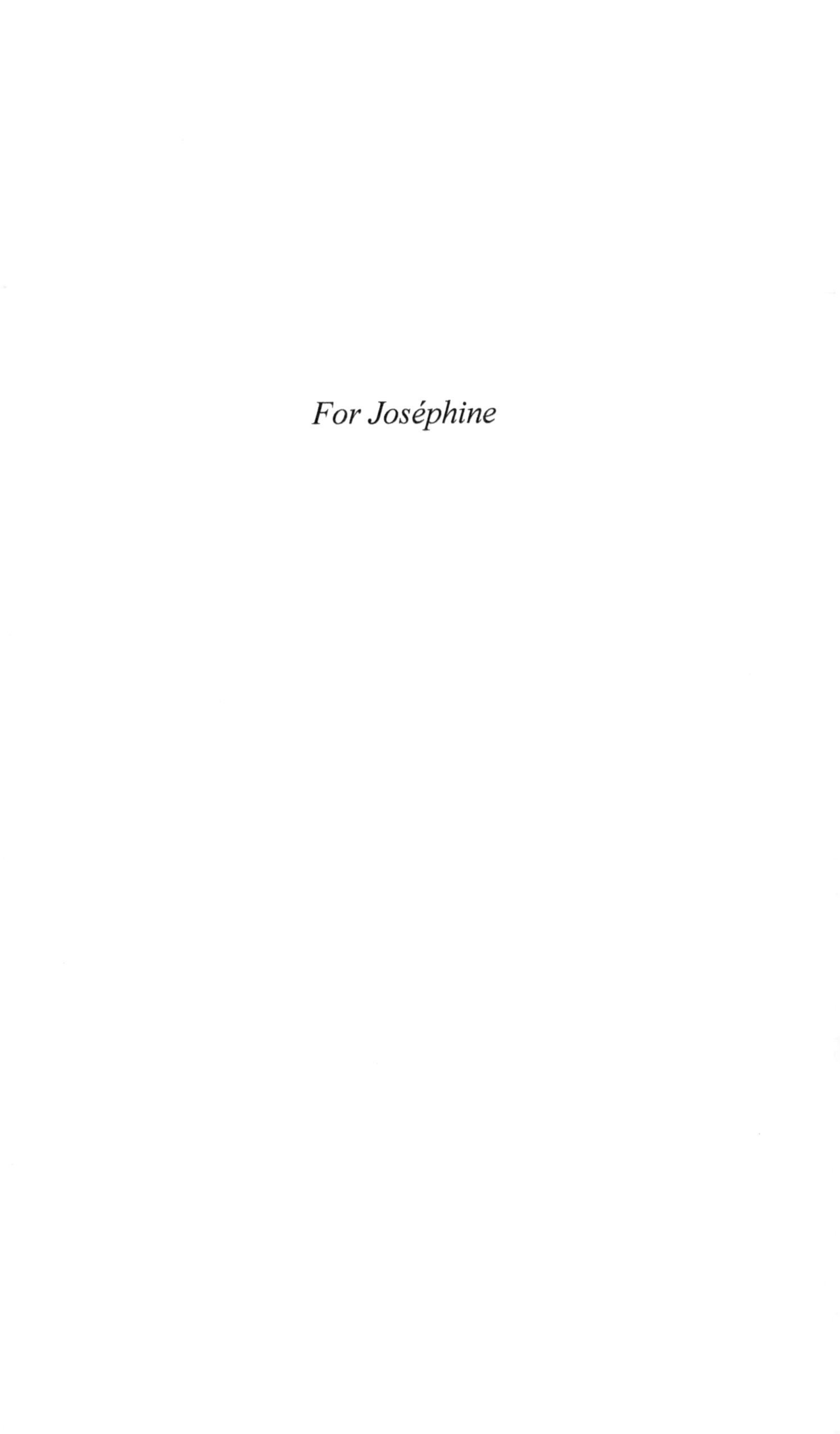

For Joséphine

CHAPTER 1

A Castle

Anna opened her eyes, sat up in a panic, and glanced at her phone. She realized she had been sleeping for almost two hours, right in the grass. Her hand flew to her face as she anxiously pressed the camera button and flipped the screen to examine her cheeks, but then she realized that she had been lying in the shade, underneath her favorite weeping willow on the castle grounds. She breathed a sigh of relief: a sunburn would certainly be unbecoming of any queen or empress. So would sleeping the afternoon away on the bare ground.

Anna stood up, took time smoothing out her hair, checking for grass stains on her pale lavender summer dress, and then stood upright, squaring her shoulders. She considered such graceful gestures to be appropriate because every time she looked out over the grounds or strolled through the halls of her new home—the Château Fleur in a small village in France—she not only felt like a royal princess but highly desired to truly be one: clad in long dresses flowing in the wind as she awaited the carriage that would take her to her royal ball, or sipping tea on the terrace overlooking the rolling hills of her kingdom.

In truth, the Château Fleur was the perfect place to have such dreams. It wasn't quite a castle—it was more of a mini-palace, a large white cube with extraordinarily high shuttered windows, little round ones in the gray-tiled roof, one small turret on the side, and acres and acres of gardens and meadows around it, all closed off by a ring of trees and an iron gate at the driveway entrance. Her bedroom had its own balcony from which she could observe the property and the rich green French countryside beyond, as a queen might survey her lands.

She was just missing the birthright.

Despite her royal ambitions, Anna knew that it wouldn't be possible for an American to claim royal ancestry in this old European country, all the more so because France had a history of disliking kings and queens, proven by their record of seizing property and beheading the royal owners. In fact, if it weren't for this lovely house and gardens, she wouldn't have wanted to live in this country at all.

Her parents had announced only a month before upending her that they were moving to France. They were finally ready to accomplish their lifelong dream of returning to that country, where they had spent their college years backpacking along the coasts of Brittany. This time, it was because they had bought Château Fleur, which they wanted to transform from the humble bed and breakfast it had been before into a more luxurious yet environmentally friendly one for foreign tourists. This strange pronouncement didn't necessarily surprise Anna: ever since her grandfather's death the year before, her father Jake had not only quit his comfortable, high-paying job in the city but also taken up a slew of strange hobbies that he claimed to have loved during his childhood: bird-calling, collecting rocks, raising ants, and constantly lecturing the family about "returning to nature."

Her mother was no better. As her obsessive beauty treatments could no longer hide all the wrinkles and sunspots she had accumulated on her cheeks over the years, she relieved her fear of aging by visiting a range of shamans, herbalists, and energetic healers—everything she had warned Anna against during her very Christian upbringing. When Anna pointed out that fact to her, her mother rolled her eyes and denied she had ever disparaged other religions or spiritual beliefs. Anna didn't pursue the matter.

She was also hardly sad to leave the middle school she had attended in the United States. After a year of being mocked incessantly for the fact that her eyebrows touched in the middle, she was excited about starting over in ninth grade.

What did make her lose sleep, apart from her almost complete lack of French, was that she would not be in the same school as her older brother. She would be going into ninth grade, which was called 3ème in French and still considered middle school. Her school would be on the other side of the village, which she could walk to every day. Luckily, it had an English section, and her mom had tried to reassure her that some of the students spoke English quite well. Henry's school would be up in the city, a train ride away. Despite his incessant teasing, Anna secretly looked up to him.

"Stop complaining again," she sighed to herself. "You know you made half your class jealous when you told them you were moving abroad. Even Lilith."

Lilith had become so jealous, in fact, that she had increased her unibrow comments to at least twice per day for the remainder of the school year, even though Anna had learned about plucking and waxing and did them on a regular basis—not because she liked it, but because she had still held out hope that it would decrease the bullying.

And so far, her summer at the château hadn't been bad. She slept in a large bedroom, in a remodeled antique canopy bed surrounded by light blue silk curtains. A shelf on the wall next to it was packed with games and books that reached up to the tall ceiling, whose original 17th-century moldings had been covered with a coat of fresh white paint and a small new chandelier attached in the middle. Her favorite part was that even with the windows open, it was always calm and quiet, except for the gentle sounds of birds and crickets.

There was also a high-walled dining room and a grand living room that still looked like it belonged in the 18th century with its twinkling chandelier, creaky wood floors, and giant fireplace. Her parents had been busy the entire summer, renovating an old library that still had all its books, the stables that hadn't been used since the 19th century, and various other rooms and hallways around the living area, as well as the grounds outside. Anna helped when asked, but she was hardly ever asked.

"Rest and enjoy your summer," her mother told her often. "You have a big year ahead of you!"

Her parents did hire her a private French tutor to keep her busy. Rose was an upbeat, kind French university student on vacation. She had grown up in the village and spoke perfect English thanks to her American mother—who was a good friend of Anna's mom and had found them the château in the first place. Rose had tutored Anna in French the entire summer, and in that short time, Anna came to see her as an older sister, with the same type of admiration she had for Henry.

Anna had spent the last few weeks exploring the grounds and even venturing into the village, which was basically deserted, as the French tended to head south or somewhere else on vacation in August, bringing most of the country to a standstill.

Anna decided to make one more round of the property before school started and see what was at the eastern end; she had never gotten around to exploring what was on the other side. It turned out to be a patch of very high grass. Delightful—she strolled through, swishing her skirt in the tall blades, then brushed her way through a small clump of trees and came out to a large meadow with even taller grass and tiny flowers of almost every color. Beyond that was a road with a vineyard on the other side.

"Perfectly quiet," she thought. Silence had been her objective these past two weeks, to counter the banging and drilling of her parents' handiwork, and her father yelling occasionally at a nail that didn't go in the right way, or a board that wouldn't stay standing.

Anna sat down on a log and her fingers twitched to her pocket. She pulled them back to her lap and folded them. She wouldn't touch her phone anymore today. Her parents had promised to transfer her a delectable amount of money into her spending account if she erased all her social media and kept her screentime minimal. It was all part of their "back to nature" regime. They checked her stats every night and released the funds little by little. Erasing the social media hadn't been hard: she had hardly had any "friends" anyway and was constantly confused by friend requests from those who belittled her in person. The followers she did have had been recruited to the eyebrow campaign in the end. The screentime was harder, though. Isolated from the world in this tiny French village, she liked to keep up with ideas for clothes and books.

"We must learn to savor the moment," Papa would say wistfully when the subject of screens came up. So she resisted the urge to pull out her phone for a picture of the vineyard. Before she could get too bored, she heard a loud car horn from the road and then saw a large black SUV come around the bend. Startled, she stopped and stared as a man in a black suit, black tie, and dark sunglasses climbed out. The car's back windows were tinted so that she couldn't see in. She wasn't used to seeing such a sight in this area. Tractors passed by more often than cars, and even though most people in the area lived comfortably, the few people she had glimpsed in town dressed for working in their gardens or horse riding.

The man approached with a kind smile, removing his sunglasses.

"Je ne vous veux pas de mal," the man said. "Je cherche le Château Fleur."

He had spoken too fast.

"Je n'ai pas compris," Anna said, gripping her skirt.

"Ah, you don't understand," said the man with an accent. "Maybe in English... I said I am not wanting to bother you. I'm looking for the Fleur Castle. The hotel."

Anna was surprised that her parents were accepting guests so soon.

"You have to turn around," she said. "Then the first right at those trees over there. There's a big iron gate. You have to use the intercom."

"Thank you!"

The man walked back to the car. While he was doing so, Anna noticed the back window rolling down. She saw the top of a summer bonnet, wrapped in a shiny rose-colored silk ribbon and decorated with a large flower of the same color. Over the edge of the window, she could just make out a pair of large, gleaming brown eyes surrounded by long, delicate eyelashes and a tall forehead. Her hand was perched on the window, and Anna noticed perfectly painted fingernails that matched the ribbon in her hat, as well as a few glimmering rings.

She had assumed that guests at the bed and breakfast would be rather well-to-do, but she had never seen anyone this young dressed so luxuriously. The mysterious passenger seemed to be Anna's age, although it was hard to tell by only seeing her face.

She looked very young, yet her eyes blazed with the confidence of someone older.

"What beautiful clothes and jewelry!" Anna said aloud, sighing. "And a private driver. Maybe she's a real future queen," Anna thought, wondering if their bed and breakfast was already that renowned.

However, Anna soon forgot about the girl as she glanced at her phone and realized that she should probably be getting home for dinner. Though her mother was immersed in her self-renewal project and the hotel, she still worried when Anna stayed out too long without saying anything. She made her way back to the château in a hurry, but not too quickly, so as not to return in an unbecoming frenzied state. Being dirty or bedraggled didn't fit with the château somehow. She paused when she reached the patio near the side entrance. The black car was waiting in the parking lot near the old stables.

"That's strange," Anna said aloud. "Client parking is across the street... this is for our home and the workers! Who could it be?"

CHAPTER 2

Rose

The next morning, Anna immediately let her eyelids close again after shutting off her alarm. She had never been an early riser (don't empresses stay in bed?), so she already couldn't wait for the first two-week vacation in October. However, a loud rap on the door jerked her completely awake.

"Mom's waiting for you, Highness. You know, school today. The Rentrée." Henry sauntered into the room, swinging his gangly teenage arms, without waiting for her answer to his knock. Surprisingly, he was already showered and dressed, and Anna marveled that his hair was actually styled and gelled for once.

"At least you knocked this time," Anna muttered. Faint morning light was starting to spill through the window and onto her white desk and the soft white carpet, then across the room to the giant fireplace on the wall opposite her bed. There was no TV in her room, and her laptop and tablet had to stay in the living room except for homework; it was part of the "no screens" package deal with her parents. She looked around at it all, sighed, then decided she couldn't deny it any longer: it was time to get up. She propped her pillow up against the headboard and herself up against the pillow. She pulled her soft, silk bedsheet up to her chin and yawned, delicately covering her mouth, then reached over to the glass on her bedside table for a tiny sip of water. More royal gestures.

Doing so reminded her of the strange evening they had had yesterday. The regal girl and her driver were nowhere to be seen, and when she had asked her parents about it at dinner, her mother had smiled, winked and told her that she would find out soon enough.

"Highness," Henry said, noticing her dainty attitude and also that her mind was starting to wander. Anna made a face, pretending to be annoyed at his nickname for her, but she secretly enjoyed it. "Mom also said to bring down your bedsheets."

Anna sighed, because bringing down one's bedsheets was not princess-like behavior.

"Fine," she said. Then, "Hey!"

Henry had gone over to her desk and grabbed a handful of pens from their holder.

"I need these for school!" he replied.

"Can't you just ask Mom to get you some new ones?" Anna sighed, sliding off the bed and beginning to gather her sheets. "You steal all my stuff."

"Nah, we start today, no time. I have a tournament to finish tonight, too." Henry was a passionate gamer. He hadn't entered into the No Screen Pact like his sister and was therefore noticeably poorer. He had been wearing the same two t-shirts all summer. He grabbed some thick books off her desk. They were graphic novels, her newfound entertainment. "And you're right, these books aren't so bad. Not as boring as those ones." He gestured to Anna's bookshelf where she kept her novels, most of which were stories that took place in the 18th and 19th centuries and featured women in delicate dresses and jewelry staring off into a beautiful landscape, clutching flowers to their hearts, or swooning into the arms of some prince. Even though romance was not one of her immediate life projects and wasn't likely to be a part of her near future anyway, she loved reading them on her balcony; they fit the Château Fleur scenery so well.

"Anyway, gotta go eat," Henry added. "Don't forget your pillowcases, too, Highness."

Anna rolled her eyes and piled the linens near the door. She was used to Henry's teasing now, which had become more frequent over the years, but deep down, her brother was kind, and she loved him nonetheless.

Anna came back to the present, and after showering, she pulled on one of her brightly colored summer dresses (she almost always wore dresses so that she could feel more royal). She particularly liked this one because she had sewn it herself. She joined her mom and brother in the kitchen.

"Did you sleep ok?" Mom asked as Anna sat down to a breakfast of French escargots aux raisins and American pancakes. When Anna had first heard the term escargots aux raisins, she had been terrified: it literally meant "snails with raisins." She had sighed in relief when she actually saw the pastry, which was similar to a cinnamon roll.

"Princess was sleeping perfectly until meanie Henry woke her up," her brother said, puffing out his lower lip to make a baby face.

Anna, forgetting her life ambition to be crowned Queen one day, pulled a raisin from a fold of her pastry and tossed it at his nose. He snatched it from the air and ate it, then poked his finger in the honey to spread it on his pancakes.

"Seriously, Henry?" Mom said, her mouth agape. "You're in high school! Now out. Your train is in twenty minutes and the walk takes 10!"

Henry swiped another escargot aux raisins, gave them a wave and disappeared into the entrance hall. As soon as was he out of their sight, a young woman in a plain green dress and a colorful bouquet tucked under her left elbow suddenly rushed into the kitchen from the other doorway.

"Carlotta!" Rose called out breathlessly. "You didn't tell them about—about—you-know-what, did you? I want to surprise her tomorrow!"

Carlotta—that is, Anna's mom—smiled at the young woman and whispered something in her ear. Rose smiled, gave a sigh of relief, handed Carlotta the bouquet, and made her way over to Anna with outstretched arms.

Anna returned the tight hug. One thing she missed in France were hugs. The French were more into kisses on the cheek as a greeting, which she was still getting used to.

"How is my Little American?" Rose said. "Are you ready for school?"

"What's the surprise?" Anna asked, ignoring Rose's questions.

"I can't tell you... but you're going to love it!" Rose exclaimed, optimistic as always, passing Anna a large bowl filled with blueberries. Then she changed the subject. "I'm sorry I haven't visited in a while."

"She has a reason," Mom said. "In fact, Rose has yet another surprise to tell you about!"

"Yes," Rose smiled, looking at Anna. "The loan was approved. Alix and I have bought the flower shop! I brought you guys a bouquet to celebrate. I'll be glad to be moving my business out of my bedroom."

"Yay!" Anna exclaimed, her eyes wide. "So you're staying here!"

Rose had talked about moving to the city to join her fiancé and it had made Anna sad.

"Yes, Little American," Rose laughed. "Alexandre will be moving here. He works online anyway. And yes, I'll still be giving you lessons when I can. And I'll see you a lot anyway because your mom was gracious enough to let us have our wedding on the lawn here at Fleur."

"I love it!" Anna exclaimed. "And—" But she was interrupted by a giant orange mass of fur that suddenly jumped onto the counter from a chair in the corner, almost upsetting her plate. Anna squealed in surprise.

"Pamplemousse!" Rose exclaimed, grabbing the cat under his large belly. She fluffed the fur on his neck and kissed him on the top of the head.

"Sorry, Anna," she said, placing him on the floor. He loped out of the kitchen and into the hallway, stopping to sniff a stack of magazines that was set to be thrown out. "I found him in the vineyards a few weeks ago in a sorry state, so I took him in. He's very sweet. But he loves the outdoors and follows me everywhere. He's more like a dog than a cat! And has the same appetite!"

"That's okay," Anna said again, thinking sadly of the dog they had left behind with her mother's friends in the U.S. "But why is he called Pamplemousse?"

"It means grapefruit," Rose said. "Because of the color."

"And the shape," Mom laughed. "He's as round as a grapefruit!"

Rose laughed too. They spent the rest of the meal discussing the flower shop and the wedding. Less than fifteen minutes later, Rose drank the last of her water, and gave Anna another hug.

"I'm off!" she said. "I have to meet up with Alix. Thanks for breakfast, Carlotta! And you—" she turned to Anna and hugged her again. "Enjoy your first day at school! I'll see you after for dinner... and a special, uh, surprise!"

CHAPTER 3

Saint Madeleine

Soon, Anna was a world away from the peace and quiet at Fleur. In fact, she wanted to throw her hands over ears, close her eyes, and teleport back to the vineyard she had seen yesterday. But she couldn't: she was standing next to her mom at the gate of the Saint Madeleine Middle School courtyard, watching what seemed like complete chaos. The space was large, between three sandy-colored cobblestone walls with tall windows. A small chapel of the same type of construction stood opposite her in the middle of the courtyard.

Everything seemed to be moving. The chapel bells were swinging, emitting a gentle but deliberate chiming sound, a few trees were lulling in the wind and kids were everywhere. Taller ones were laughing and shoving each other around in little groups, smaller students were racing through them. Some girls were crouched over a phone, swaying to the music. A few were somehow kicking around a soccer ball in the middle of it all and Anna wondered if there were often students or teachers who took a ball to the head. In fact, the general atmosphere wasn't much different than the wait times at her old school, but something in the way the kids acted was.

There was the French, of course. Anna didn't understand anything of the conversations she overheard, and in the background, there were shouts of sweet words that Rose had warned her not to say in front of teachers. Girls kissed each other on cheeks, and boys reached out as if to shake hands but instead tapped their palms together in greeting. Except for the colorful sneakers, it seemed as if almost everyone was dressed in one of three colors: black or gray.

"Ready?" Anna's mom broke from her moment of quiet observation. "She should be here any minute."

Rose's mom personally knew the principal and had asked her to see to it that Anna was comfortable on the first day. Madame Braun was supposed to meet them in the courtyard. As they waited, the church bells stopped and a twinkly music played out over the intercom. After another wash of movement, Anna was surprised to see sudden order—compared to the chaos she had just witnessed, anyway—descend upon the students.

The noise level remained the same, but the older kids arranged themselves into casual lines on the left side of the courtyard, smaller kids in front of the chapel and the tiniest—Anna supposed they were the sixth-graders, or *6ème*, to the right. She was surprised that they knew exactly where to go on the first day, then realized there were markings on the ground—numbers.

What's my number? She wondered.

"Anna, Anna!"

As the kids filed into class, each line behind an adult, a portly woman in heels, black stockings, a flowy blue dress and plenty of gold jewelry approached Anna. The woman held out her hand to her mother.

"I am Madame Braun," she said. "It is so nice to meet you. Welcome to Saint Madeleine."

Anna sighed in relief. Madame Braun's English was great.

"Thanks so much for coming!" Mom answered. She sounded so overly enthusiastic compared to the serious woman in front of her. "Anna is so excited to be here, but a little nervous too, aren't you?"

Anna tore her eyes away from two boys throwing a ball of paper at another one, hidden from their teacher at the end of the line.

"Oh yes," she said. "Excited. But I hardly speak French..."

"Rose has told me that you make great progress," the principal said. "And it is no matter. This is why I will today accompany you to class."

Anna's mind wandered as they began to walk together. She suddenly felt no bigger than a sixth grader.

Ridiculous, she told herself. *Ninth graders are the oldest in middle school. Chin up.*

Madame Braun was pointing out some features of the courtyard: where the door for the offices and classrooms were, where the cafeteria was, and where Anna should line up in the morning. They mystery of her number was solved: she would be in classroom 222 with her *prof principal.*

"Your *prof principal* is like your homeroom teacher for the class. You have one *classe*, or group of students that you will do all your classes with. So if you don't know where to go, just follow them."

The same group of students all day? Anna frowned. Even in middle school in the US, she had had some classes, like Spanish, with kids from other groups. And she thought longingly of her classmates back in the U.S. who would be choosing their own classes in ninth grade.

"I guess if we don't like each other, we're stuck together," she mumbled to her mom.

Her mom frowned at her.

"But if you love each other, you'll be together all day," Carlotta said, with her usual positivity. "Anna, you'll be fine. I've got to go. Call me if you need me."

Madame Braun stopped.

"No phones in middle school," she said, pointing to a sign that was just above where Anna had seen the girls dancing earlier. Madame Braun saw the look on Anna's face and said, "It's a national law. But you can go to the *Vie Scolaire* over there and ask in case of emergency. I told them you are here. It is rather small here, so we know everyone."

When her mom had squeezed her daughter's arm and taken her leave, Anna followed the principal up some stone steps, through a large wooden door, and into a wooden-floored hallway. The walls were covered in a display of student artwork: portraits of royal and historical figures made from bits of confetti. One of them caught her eye: a young princess, maybe, with a rose-colored silk ribbon in her hair and flowers of the same color all over her dress. That and the gleaming, confident brown eyes reminded her of the girl in the mysterious car yesterday. Anna didn't have much time to think about her, though. Madame Braun had reached the classroom.

The confidence of royalty, she reminded herself, thinking of a certain summer day with Rose.

CHAPTER 4

Conversations

"Describe a time when you were... *heureuse*," Rose widened her eyes and flashed an overexaggerated smile. It was June and Anna had only been in a France for a few weeks.

"*Heureuse*... happy, right?" Anna asked. Rose nodded.

"Ma mère dis-moi nous allons en un château !"

"Not bad," Rose said. "Ma mère m'a dit qu'on allait vivre dans un château."

This was the way Anna was learning French. Rose would ask questions, Anna would answer, Rose would correct and then explain after. They were stretched out in lawn chairs in broad-brimmed summer hats, sipping endless *sirop de menthe*, a sweet mix of cold water and minty syrup that Anna had become quite addicted to.

"You were happy to come here?" Rose asked. "Tu n'avais pas peur?"

"*Peur...*" Anna took another sip of sirop to buy time. "Fear! No. Not really. I wasn't too happy, though, until I found out about the castle. And I guess I was happy to leave my school. *Heureuse quitter mon école américaine.*"

"J'étais contente de quitter mon école américaine," she said. "Et tes amis ?"

Anna blushed. *Amis* meant friends and it hadn't been her area of specialty.

Rose seemed to notice the reddening of Anna's cheeks underneath her hat.

"Did I say something wrong?"

"No, no," Anna said. "But you know, my family moved around a lot. I didn't have time to make friends at my last school."

That was only a half-truth. She had had three years to make friends, but Lilith had made sure she didn't make any permanent ones. Rose didn't answer but her soft eyes met Anna's. They didn't hold pity but something about them seemed open and attentive, as if reassuring Anna that it was okay to think out loud.

"Maybe it was my fault though," Anna said. "I didn't like the same things as they did. They thought it was cool to drink and have boyfriends, but I didn't want to, and my parents would have killed me anyway. For some reason, that made them mad."

Rose nodded and Anna realized she needed to get it out. That knot in her stomach that she had had since everyone had joined the Lilith Regime was still there but loosening with every word she spoke.

"Someone ripped up the dresses I had made for history class. It was for a contest too, and the teacher was sure I would win. They were miniatures but it had taken me three months to make. I even sewed all the miniature flowers and beaded all the pearls that I attached to them. My grandma taught me how to sew, you know. She even gave me her sewing machine just before she passed away. One of the dresses had a long train of roses. Look—" she pulled out her phone and pulled up pictures of her sewing projects. She handed the phone to Rose, who swiped thoughtfully through the album.

"Someone cut them off and then took a picture of the dress and called them 'doll dresses' and put it online," Anna continued. "And I was like... afraid to go to school but... like... we don't have the choice." She realized she had been talking fast and was running out of breath. She put down her glass harder than she had intended, and some green liquid splashed onto the metal coffee table.

Rose looked up from the phone and handed it back. Her eyes hadn't changed, and with a knot in her stomach, Anna realized why she had never told her parents about the bullying. They had never looked at her with those attentive eyes.

As if reading her mind, Rose said, "Didn't you tell the teacher? Your parents?"

"My parents were sad about grandpa," Anna sighed. "I didn't want to make it worse for them. And I didn't know the teachers too well."

Rose rolled on to her side.

"T'inquiète pas," Rose said. "Don't worry. They were probably just jealous of you. That's really cool that you can sew!"

Anna shrugged. It had felt good to finally talk about it, and she wanted to say more, but she didn't want Rose feeling sorry for her either.

Maybe I am weird, she thought. *And I'd rather Rose not know right away.*

"Actually, they were probably just jealous because you had passions and hobbies and they were just doing boring, stupid things," Rose said. "I had the same problem in high school. A girl really hated that I was obsessed with gardening. My mom told me she was just jealous that I had the confidence to do something different."

"So kids here are the same?" Anna asked, the knot suddenly returning.

"No, no," Rose said. "Just a few, but everyone ends up hating them in the end. And anyway, if you're just confident in yourself, you'll be fine. I saw your history books. Kings and Queens, Emperors and Empresses..."

Anna blushed. "Lilith said they were stupid."

"Lilith is a peasant who doesn't live in a castle," Rose said, gesturing back to the house, and Anna laughed.

"Anyway," Rose continued. "Whether they were loved or hated, the royalty all had self-confidence. Some were arrogant, probably, but at least they never doubted themselves. They were brought up to believe they were almost divine. The confidence of royalty."

"The confidence of royalty," Anna repeated aloud. She liked the way it sounded. The knot in her stomach was gone now and the sun was getting hotter, making her drowsy. They hadn't done much French today, but it didn't matter.

"About those dresses," Rose said. "Do you still have them?"

"Uh... yeah. Mom kept them in a trunk. She has them up on the top floor somewhere, I think. Why?"

"That would be a nice vintage decoration for my shop, if we get our loan," Rose said. "Or the flowers you made—yeah, that would be cool! We could even sell cloth bouquets. What do you think? I'll give you half the profits."

She held out her hand.

Anna smiled and took it. If Rose wanted them for her shop, where people would see them, maybe they weren't so silly after all.

"Great," Rose said, rolling back on her back and closing her eyes at the ever-brightening sun. "Now let's take a nap."

Anna liked that idea. But first, she glanced the castle across the lawn and imagined a Lady opening the shutters, dressed in a flowering blue ball gown enlaced with pearls. The Lady stared dreamily into the distance, stroked her hair, aware of her own beauty and importance, then reached to the side, picked up a basket and dumped some laundry out of the window. It landed in a heap on Lilith's head. Anna smiled. *The confidence of royalty.*

CHAPTER 5

Abeni

Anna's mind flew back to the present. About thirty students were waiting in the classroom, two or three each at small rectangle tables, standing with their hands folded in front of them and looking directly at her. Anna took a deep breath and forced herself to look at the walls to avoid the attention. Her hands clenched up against her skirt. She wasn't necessarily shy, but she'd rather go unnoticed if she had the choice. The last time she had put herself out there at school—winning the school spelling bee against the supposed smartest girl in the school—it had led to not much more than an ugly plastic trophy and plenty more comments about her eyebrows.

The classroom was simple, with a few posters clinging to the yellow walls. The floorboards creaked as she followed the principal to a step at the front of the room so that she was next to the teacher's desk. The entire front part of the room was elevated, and the projector screen dangled from the tall ceiling, hiding most of the green chalkboard behind it. The projector seemed out of place in this classroom that looked like the ones she had seen in old movies. Anna glanced up at the projector, then her eyes fell on the other adult on the opposite side of the desk. She too was standing with her hands folded in front of her, her large green eyes kind but her mouth unsmiling. She looked at Madame Braun and said something quickly in French.

Then she turned to Anna and said, "Welcome. We have chance to have you at this college. It is evidence. Questions are not grave, just lift your main. I am so good in English."

Anna's eyes widened. She knew that the teacher was speaking English, and her accent wasn't bad, but she hadn't exactly understood everything.

Madame Braun cleared her throat and leaned over to Anna.

"She means to say that we are *lucky* to have you at this *middle school*. It's *obvious*. If you have questions, it's not *a problem*, just raise your *hand*." She smiled slightly, the first time Anna had seen her do so, and leaned towards Anna. "Sometimes, English and French get mixed up a little, when words sound the same."

Then she straightened up and her face went stone-serious again.

"Madame Marel is your *professeur principal*," Madame Braun explained, loud enough for the rest of the class to hear. "That means she is the head teacher of the class, and you can come to her for help or questions about the school. She's also your math teacher. She just said that you are very welcome in class and that we are lucky to have you here." Then she looked up at the class and addressed them in a formal tone.

"Bonjour les 33. Bienvenue en troisième. Cette année, on a une nouvelle élève. Elle s'appelle Anna et elle vient de l'Amérique. Elle parle un peu de français mais je compte sur vous de faire en sorte qu'elle se sent la bienvenue."

Anna knew just enough to enough French to understand that Madame Braun was welcoming them to ninth grade and introducing Anna from America. She recognized the word *bienvenue* meaning *welcome* and it made her feel a bit better. Whispers broke out across the classroom and Anna saw that some of the students' eyes widened. A small boy in the front with freckles and a large mass of curly hair startled and the mess of books, papers and pens on his desk fell to the floor. A tall girl in the front row with shiny straight brown hair, a sparkly white t-shirt, jeans and chunky white sneakers leaned over to her left and whispered something to the girl next to her. They didn't take their eyes off her either, but Anna couldn't tell if they were amazed, puzzled or judgmental. It didn't matter. So many others were smiling at her, especially the freckled boy, and Anna's hands relaxed a little.

Madame Braun cleared her throat and the noise ceased immediately.

"Where is Abeni?"

A thin girl in the front row with rich brown eyes, curly black hair, and small, round red glasses raised her hand.

"I've spoken with Abeni's parents, and yours too," Madame Braun explained to Anna. "Abeni speaks four languages, including English, and she's lived in a few different places all over the world."

Abeni smiled kindly and pushed her loose glasses up the bridge of her nose.

"She is your translator for the teachers who don't speak English too well," Madame Braun continued. "I explain to the class that you are the only ones who have the right to chat during class—in a low whisper, of course! Your teachers know this, too."

She said a few more things in French to the class and Anna could just make out that Madame Braun was to return that afternoon to accompany them to the chapel. Then she showed Anna an empty desk next to Abeni.

"Do not worry, Anna," Madame Braun said, her rigid demeanor softening again. "I taught French for two years in San Francisco. I know that school is different in the two countries. If you have any problems, please speak to Madame Marel, and she will send you to me if you need more help. You are in the international section, so the class speaks relatively good English for their age... well, they're supposed to."

Anna smiled and nodded but was still too nervous to speak.

Then the principal left, and Madame Marel went behind her desk to consult her computer.

"Adelbert, Chloé," she called out.

The girl in the sparkly white t-shirt raised her hand gently and purposefully, and said, "Présent!" before pulling out her chair, sitting down and folding her hands in front of her in rapt attention, a satisfied smile on her lips.

"Beaufils, Victoire," Madame Marel continued. The girl next to Chloé, dressed almost the same, responded and sat down.

"Mahkatooranna" the teacher called out after reading a few more names. There was a brief silence. Madame Marel stared straight at Anna, waiting, and Abeni nudged her in the side.

"Mikotooranna," Madame Marel repeated. "Anna, is you."

"Oui," she answered, and sat down quickly, feeling silly even though she knew the teacher hadn't even come close to pronouncing her name correctly.

Abeni raised her hand. "Madame, si je peux me permettre, je crois que ça se prononce MacArthur, son nom de famille. MacArthur, Anna."

Anna heard her last name and understood that Abeni had corrected the teacher's pronunciation of Anna's last name. Madame Marel nodded and continued.

When she said, "Trebuche, Gabin," the small, freckled boy answered, "Quoi? Euh... present!" and almost fell over into his seat.

Madame Marel finished the roll call, then looked up at Anna.

"Close the store, please, Anna."

Anna stared at her.

"Um... which store?" she asked. She couldn't imagine why the teacher was asking her to shut down a shop.

Abeni elbowed her gently and grinned. "I think she means the window shades next to you. *Store* means 'the shade' in English."

Anna did as she was told and then looked gratefully at Abeni. She decided she liked her translator. She seemed authentic, fashionable but also just the right level of awkward—much like herself.

Madame Marel noticed the girls exchanging a look.

"This year will be formidable for Anna with you as our translator," she said.

"*Formidable* means great," Abeni whispered with a smirk when the teacher had turned her back on them again.

In any case, they would be sure to laugh together, Anna thought, stifling a giggle.

CHAPTER 6

A Guest

"You're in 3ème now," Madame Marel announced when everyone was seated. "Do not expect this year to be as easy as the last ones. You have your *Brevet* next year!"

"What is *Brevet*?" Anna whispered to Abeni as they stood behind their desks at the front and waiting for the signal to sit down.

"The exam at the end of 3ème which will decide which type of high school we can go to," Abeni whispered back. "My older brother says it's a joke, but I think it sounds scary."

Anna's stomach dropped when Madame Marel handed out the schedules and she saw that she wouldn't finish until five o'clock p.m. every day. There was no class on Wednesday afternoon, like the previous years, but the other days of the week seemed longer.

"17h means 5 p.m.," Abeni told her when she saw Anna's wide-eyed look, which usually meant she hadn't understood something in French.

"Yes, I know," Anna said. She had gotten used to the French way of using military time for schedules. "But it's so late, and—" but Madame Marel had begun to speak. Anna didn't want to lose points in her *carnet de correspondence,* the booklet that the teacher was now distributing. Anna knew that it in this booklet the teacher could write notes to parents, and she could lose points for bad behavior, or also earn points occasionally for good deeds. Rose had mentioned that over the summer.

As Anna began to glue her schedule into the back of the booklet as instructed, she noticed Chloé staring at her, her eyes sweeping up and down her outfit, and not in a kindly way. Anna felt a strange urge to throw a large blanket over her body and fixed her eyes on her booklet, but not before noticing that Chloé was wearing almost the exact same outfit as Abeni, just a little brighter and with a better ironing job.

In fact, Chloé and her friend Victoire didn't participate when several students surrounded Anna and Abeni in the courtyard after they were let go at the end of the day.

"Gabin wants to know if you actually met Nella," Abeni had said, translating a question from the tiny, freckled boy in the group of students who crowded around her and Anna. He had spoken too fast, and fidgeted his hands too much when he spoke, so Anna needed help understanding him.

"Nella?"

"You know, the influencer," Abeni said.

"The whole school dresses like her now," Delphine said, sweeping her hand from her hip to show off her outfit... which did look exactly like Chloé's and Abeni's.

"And do you eat Burger King every day?" Inès, a very blonde-haired girl with colorful sneakers to contrast her all-black outfit, piped up. "They just open one here, it is one hour to go!"

"Your life is so much fairy tale," Delphine sighed.

Anna smiled kindly at her. "Yours is too, Delphine. You live in France!"

"France is... how do you say... *nase*?" Delphine asked Abeni.

"Lame," Abeni said, then continued in French: "But how can you say that? Isn't your family descended from dukes and duchesses, Delphine?"

Anna realized she was started to grasp the French conversations more easily. Plus, her classmates were starting to figure out that if they spoke slowly and clearly, she could understand.

"Well, France doesn't have dukes and duchesses anymore, so who cares," Delphine sighed.

Anna remembered something she had read in a book that summer.

"It would be easy to be a princess if I were dressed in cloth of gold, but it is a great deal more of a triumph to be one all the time when no one knows it," she told Delphine, hoping that her translation into French had been accurate.

Gabin cocked his head to the side, looking puzzled as usual. Delphine and Inès nodded as if they were impressed even though their wide eyes evoked confusion, and Anna grinned wider, proud of her ability to memorize lines even if no one else was... until she noticed that Chloé, standing a bit off to the side of their circle with her friend Victoria, was outright rolling her eyes. Then Chloé and Victoria looked at each other, suppressed a laugh and went back to secretly typing on their smartphones hidden halfway in their matching bright silver handbags. They only stopped when Madame Braun approached. They quickly dropped their devices into the bags, folding their hands politely in front of them and flashing the principal innocent smiles at exactly the same time as she passed by.

Anna knew those expressions and reactions. She had seen them at her old school. Before she could give them any more thought, the young teens were shooed towards the gate by the *surveillant* who was responsible for monitoring the courtyard during recess and after school.

Anna's mom was waiting for her on the stone steps of the château, still in her gardening outfit, a gooey pale-white paste smothered on her cheeks and forehead. She gestured at the girls to come through the gate.

"Come meet the witch doctor," Anna told Abeni. "If you want better grades, she probably has a face mask for it."

"Aloe vera to lift my face," Carlotta called out as they approached. "Would you like one? I didn't use the whole plant myself."

"We're good," Anna said. "Trust me," she added to Abeni, who was grinning. "It gets messy." Her mother pretended not to hear.

"Come sit. You must be the Abeni that Rose told me about." She beckoned to the garden table and chairs with their swirling metal designs in front of the living room window. Some glasses, ice water and a bottle of green *sirop*, plus some biscuits, were ready for them. "How was the first day of school?"

The girls sat and Anna told her Mom about their curious questions from her classmates.

"They love America then," Mom laughed. "I guess you're the star!"

"She is," said Abeni. "They were talking about her all day long. We've been more or less in the same class with the same people and the same teachers for three years now. Finally something exciting is happening here!"

Anna smiled. She thought of her summer conversation with Rose and decided that school might not be so bad here after all, and that even if the others never accepted her as royalty, they at least wouldn't look down on her.

"And do you like your teachers?" Mom continued.

Anna and Abeni shared a glance.

"They're kind, I suppose," Anna said. "But some are super-serious, like Monsieur Beauharnais. He teaches history."

"Yeah," Abeni piped up. "We can't talk for the whole hour, except when he passes out papers, or to answer a question! Three kids already lost points in their *carnet*. He wouldn't even lend Gabin a pen and wrote him up for it... on the first day! And he always drops the eraser. And Madame Marel is verrrrrry confident in her English!"

After some more chit-chat, Anna's mom seemed relieved and announced that she had to harvest the borage flowers for her anti-wrinkle after-dinner tea that night.

Anna showed Abeni back to the gate then went inside and dropped her bags in the den next to the living room. She liked this cozy room for doing homework or reading. It was lined with bookshelves, and the previous owner had left quite a few dusty and ancient volumes on the shelves. She had moved in some of her own as well, and she always kept a stack of her current reads on the sturdy oak coffee table in front of the fireplace, which was smaller than the one in the living room and had a fake furnace inside. She would always settle into the refurbished Louis XV armchair that made her feel like she had sat down into another century.

She already had homework—Monsieur Beauharnais was very generous in this area. He had probably realized that written homework at home could be done by artificial intelligence and sought to make up for that fact by not sparing the quantity.

"Busy work," Anna grumbled and by the time she finished translating, organizing notes, researching and re-translating it, it was almost eight o'clock—French dinner time.

"We have a special guest tonight," Mom said, popping her head into the den. "Rose's surprise! I think you're going to make another great friend!"

Anna was intrigued and followed her mom to the dining room. Rose and Henry were sitting at a large wooden table. They had their backs to the tall stone fireplace, and on the other wall was a large glass window that overlooked the park in front of the castle. In the corner of the room was a large, shiny grand piano with an old orange and gold tapestry hanging on the wall behind it. It featured knights and royal ladies. Mom had explained that it was a copy of a famous

French tapestry, but still quite expensive, that had been offered to them by the former owner as a thank-you for restoring the château to its former likeness—he had been leery about selling to Americans who might put their own twist on things, he had told the realtor.

Tonight, however, it wasn't the tapestry, nor the grand window, nor the elegant piano that attracted her attention. Sitting on one side of the table, surrounded by a halo of light from the sunset illuminating the glass windows, was a prim young girl with bright brown eyes, perfectly painted fingernails, and fingers covered in rings that glinted in the light of the falling sun.

CHAPTER 7

The Girl From California

"Anna, this is my cousin Olivia," Rose said. "She's visiting from California this week and couldn't wait to meet you!"

Olivia was wearing a matching shiny green silk dress with lace across the chest and a lace ribbon in her shiny hair. The ends of her ponytail were twisted into neat curls that flowed down her back. A white flower was tucked behind her ear. Like Rose, her dark hair faded into light brown dye near the ends. She was waiting with her hands and their perfectly painted nails folded in front of her, and she was staring straight at Anna, who suddenly became very aware of her own unpainted fingernails, the summer dress which Chloé had looked at with disgust and straight, flat hair that had become slightly tangled in the breeze on the patio.

Olivia smiled and gave a cheerful, "Hi!", but Anna couldn't help feeling that her own appearance was quite dull compared to Rose's cousin. She returned the greeting with a small smile.

"Olivia lives near Los Angeles!" Mom said. "I went there many years ago and there's nothing like it."

"My Dad married my mom there," Rose explained. "Olivia's here to visit but also to help me with the shop and the wedding and basically everything I have going on this year," Rose grinned, as she always did when speaking of her project.

"She's very good at the piano," Carlotta added, "and is going to play at the ceremony."

"Her parents have invested a little in the store," Rose went on cheerfully. "And I suspect they sent Olivia to make sure I'm spending their money wisely!"

"Probably, but of course I'll tell them only good things," Olivia said with a sweet smile. "I just want to be with my favorite cousin! And it will be an honor to play music for you."

"I wish you were young enough to be flower girl," Rose sighed. "You always have a perfect flower in your hair." She poked the silk flower in Olivia's hair tie.

"How about a Junior Bridesmaid?" Mom suggested.

Olivia and Rose smiled affectionately at each other, and Anna could see that they were more than just cousins. Suddenly, Olivia's soft and prim way of speaking suddenly irked her. Then her chest felt tight, and she realized that a strange feeling was welling up in it... was it jealousy? She had spent the summer with Rose, who had always been kind to her, but Rose looked at Olivia not just with kindness but something else. Admiration?

"Olivia is staying with me. She's just here for tonight," Rose said. "We're leaving again for Paris tomorrow and we'll be back next weekend. I've been taking her around the region for the last few days...or rather, her driver has been bringing us everywhere."

"You have your own driver?" Henry said to Olivia. "So cool. So California."

"Not everyone in LA has a driver, Henry," Anna said, rolling her eyes.

"Yes, my family is fortunate to be able to pay for one," Olivia said, articulating every sound and syllable in that annoying way.

"Can he drive me to the city this weekend?" Henry asked, his eyes wide.

Mom frowned at him. "You're going to be studying this weekend, young man."

"Oh come oooon," Henry said, looking imploringly at Olivia.

"Well, like I said, we're leaving tomorrow," Rose repeated. In fact, Anna realized that Henry had been staring so admiratively at Olivia that he had missed this piece of information the first time Rose had said it. "And then Olivia has a concert in Paris with the Youth

Orchestra and a promotional event in Bordeaux and some other engagements. And then don't worry, Henry, she'll be back here from time to time throughout the school year."

"I'm doing online school this year," Olivia said. "But I would love to make some French friends. And if the village is my home base during my stay in France, I can help Rose with the shop and the wedding, too."

Rose and Olivia beamed at each other again.

They continued the meal, listening as Mom and Rose talked about the shop: which color the shelves on the sidewalk in front of the shop would be, if they should match the curtains, and other details. Olivia pitched in from time to time with her own ideas—she had already been to some grandiose weddings in California with the world's top floral designers, she explained.

Then the adults went into the kitchen with the plates and in search of dessert.

Olivia reached down and pulled up a smooth green handbag with pink flowers splashed across the front. She placed it on the table and pulled out a large smartphone.

"Let's take a picture together," she said to Anna and Henry. "I want to show my followers my new friends in France!"

She came to the other side of the table and stuck her head between their shoulders. Anna hardly had time to smile before Olivia snapped the picture.

"Look," Olivia said, typing away at the screen, sliding some filters over the image, then showing it to Anna. "I posted it."

"Wow," Henry said, staring over her shoulder. "You have so many followers!"

Olivia shrugged. "That's because of my piano. I write music myself. But I also like to post pictures of my travels and some fashion, too." She showed the picture to Anna again. "Don't we look great?"

Anna smiled at her, then took a few sips of water. In truth, she felt quite embarrassed that others would see that picture. It highlighted Olivia's beautiful clothes and hair and huge smile, which Anna could see she didn't have herself. She wasn't from California and didn't have a driver either. She also couldn't play the piano. And social media had been a failure. *Maybe that's why Rose looks at her differently than she looks at me*, Anna thought, *because everything about her is cool and pretty and perfect. Royal.*

When Anna went upstairs to her room that night, she glanced at her phone for the first time since that morning. Abeni had sent her some of Nella's videos. She watched all five of them, hardly caring that her daily usage would mean subtractions from her bank account, then glanced at her closet. Through the open door, she saw her colorful summer dresses and sighed. *Those don't look cool either,* she thought.

Then she noticed one of her old dolls with her handmade dress was stashed deeply into a corner. Despite her past disappointment with sewing, Anna drew it out. It had been one of her favorites, and one of the only ones that hadn't been damaged, so she hadn't stored it away in the attic at their old house. The brown-eyed doll, with her glistening deep pink gown and pearl jewelry, reminded her of Olivia. Olivia didn't dress like Nella, but something about her outfits seemed even more fashionable than Chloé and Abeni's—like a modern twist on 19th-century fashion.

I had the idea first, Anna grumbled, and placed the doll far back in the closet.

CHAPTER 8

Queen of Saint Madeleine

Anna was starting to understand that what she wore didn't matter to most of her classmates. She was becoming, as her mom had said, a star. Gabin, Delphine and Inès sought her out at every recess, asking questions about American cities, celebrities, and schools. They helped with her French and explained the food in the cafeteria.

"Where's the ketchup?" Anna asked the day that fries were being served.

"Just mayonnaise," Gabin grinned, dousing his pile of fries with some.

Anna's mouth dropped open in horror.

"Mayonnaise on fries?"

"Soooo good," said Delphine.

"Yeah, the French do that," Abeni laughed.

Anna especially liked her English classes with a teacher named Miss Rabhi, who was new at the school this year. She spoke English with a posh British accent. Miss Rabhi not only used the most exciting interactive games in class, but she also let them play on the tablets and had even set the class up with pen pals with whom they could video call during certain classes. Anna was allowed to read during this time, because even though she was in the international section, she was still much more advanced than her classmates. English class was three times per week. She was glad to have a break from the hum of French that she had to concentrate on all day to understand even a few words.

In her other classes, Anna had tried to keep up with taking notes. She sometimes got tired halfway through a lesson and found it hard to continue listening to the French, so she would wait patiently until Abeni finished copying hers or asked her to translate them on the strange sheets of paper that looked like a grid with many crisscrossing blue lines. She still wasn't used to the paper, either, as she had grown up using American sheets with just simple blue lines and the vertical red line on the left. Strange how even the smallest details were different in this country, she thought.

When Anna was tired, she didn't feel confident speaking French and therefore refrained from participating; in English class, however, she raised her hand to answer every question, which of course were not difficult to understand or answer, even when she was sleepy.

"You must be the American," Miss Rabhi had said to her on the first day. "Maybe you can be my assistant. Why don't you come to the front, and we can make a dialogue out of the paragraph we just read."

For once, Anna didn't mind being in front of the others, since she knew she couldn't make a mistake.

"Which qualities do you admire most in superheroes?" Miss Rabhi said loudly and clearly.

"Strength, physical and mental," Anna said, speaking slowly for the benefit of the others.

"And Gabin, which qualities do you admire most in superheroes?"

Gabin's eyes widened, then looked left and right.

"Yes?" he said. Anna grinned. Gabin answered "yes" to anything in English.

"Let's try again," Miss Rabhi frowned.

When they went on to their writing exercises, students clambered to be Anna's group. She always chose Abeni, Gabin, Delphine and Inès, of course. Gabin even ignored some snickers from her classmates when he rushed to sit next to her.

"They're friends," Abeni said, rolling her eyes at the group of boys behind her. "Boys," she muttered, turning back to Anna. Anna didn't mind. And despite the laughs, she knew those boys, too, would be asking her questions about the assignment in a few minutes, as well as other students from the class, except for Chloé and Victoire. Madame Rabhi even allowed Anna to make rounds to the other groups to help them correct their work.

"Your accent is so cool," said Lena, a beautiful girl who was even more stylish than Chloé.

Chloé and Victoire might see clothes, Anna realized, but the rest of the class didn't. They seemed in awe and admiration of her, and Anna was quite enjoying it. She didn't care about Olivia anymore. The Californian might impress her family, but at school, Anna was Queen.

CHAPTER 9

The Picnic

The next weekend came quickly. After spending long school days inside and Saturday translating her notes, Anna was glad when Mom announced a picnic atop Saint Madeleine Hill with Henry, Rose, and Olivia, who was back from her trip. At noon on Sunday, they met Rose and Olivia in front of the future flower shop. It wasn't much to look at for now: dust from peeling red paint around the dusty windows fluttered away in the breeze and the old name of the butcher shop—Boucherie Moulin-Frères—was still visible above the doorway.

It made Anna smiled to think of Rose outside, placing colorful flowerpots on shelves to interest passers-by on a sunny Saturday morning, with smells of roses in the air. But today, the breeze floating past only smelled of leaves starting to dry out for fall, which wasn't so bad either. Anna sat down on the steps in front of the old butcher shop and breathed it in while her Mom and Henry peeked in the window of the jewelry shop next door, which also looked like it had been abandoned for quite some time.

Anna felt a renewed sense of confidence today: she wouldn't even mind the Olivia's presence this time, because she had made efforts to dress just as nicely, donning her best short-sleeve white lace dress that she had tied off with a satin pink ribbon, tugging the skirt up into it to make it shorter. She had also decided to go back to wearing jewelry: she had put on a necklace, earrings and as many rings as she owned—four in total.

It was the closest she could come to Olivia's style, and she didn't care that Henry had told her it made her look like a bride on *Married in 20 Minutes*.

As they waited, the black SUV with tinted back windows approached and stopped in front of her. Rose and Olivia each popped halfway out.

When Anna saw them, her heart sank. All her efforts to dress like royalty had been in vain. Olivia was wearing a perfectly white summer dress with a ruffled taffeta skirt and a light blue satin ribbon around her waist. The ribbon and flowers in her summer bonnet matched her belt perfectly, as did the shiny handbag she was carrying on her wrist, a small light blue handbag with white daffodils on the front pocket. Even the orange

Pamplemousse nestled in her arms seemed to match the ensemble. Anna realized that she didn't own a single purse, whereas Olivia seemed to have one to match every dress she owned. The purses themselves were beautiful, in shiny materials or neat leather, and even Chloé didn't own such perfect-looking bags.

Next time we go shopping, Anna thought, glancing down at her six-year-old faded white shoulder bag. *I'll ask Mom for a leather purse. Definitely more sleek.*

"Climb in," Rose said to Anna, pointing to the car. Olivia smiled at Anna, who smiled back stiffly, and couldn't help but marvel that Olivia had this car to herself on a regular basis. It was spacious inside, large television screens on the backs of the leather seats in front of them and cold drinks with sparkling glasses lined up in holders along the door.

"Wow, this is nice!" Henry exclaimed, searching for how to turn on the screens. Anna preferred to stare out the window, avoiding Olivia's eyes. She didn't know what to do or say anyway. She had never been in such a fine car. Rose clambered in the front and chatted with the driver as the car turned out of the park and into the dusty country road leading away from the château and towards the hills in the distance.

Before starting the climb up St. Madeleine Hill, the driver unpacked a large picnic basket from the trunk and asked Rose if she wanted him to carry it up for her, which she gratefully accepted.

"Follow me, everyone," she said. "You'll see. The view at the top is beautiful!"

She led the way, followed by the driver then Olivia, who had begun a conversation with Henry about the part of the movie he had watched in the car. Anna followed closely behind, listening for a while, then letting her mind wander to the scenery unfolding around her as they made their way up a winding path, Pamplemousse at their heels.

She could make out the school and church in the distance, with the green field behind it. Beyond the school were the red-tile roofs of neat little houses. They were clumped together around the winding streets, but at the edge of the village, they became more and more spread out, intermingled with white blockish villas until only one or two dotted the hilly landscape with its lazily grazing cows and horses. She couldn't see her home from here, but she was sure that the château was one of the largest properties in the village, and its grounds the size of two or three farms; she wondered how much bigger Olivia's must be and as she was thinking it, she heard Mom exclaim. "Three swimming pools! Wow!"

"Like a Royal Highness," Henry said. "Can I call you that?"

Anna didn't hear Olivia's answer, but as they turned around a rock that marked a bend on the path, Anna stopped, not only because she was started to tire, but also because she was starting to feel angry. *Highness*!

She had pretended to be annoyed by Henry's nickname for herself but couldn't stand to hear him give it to someone else.

Everyone thinks Olivia's so cool, Anna thought. *Mom, Henry, Rose... I'm still here, guys!*.

She continued on her way, feeling gloomy despite the ever-brightening sun. Finally, they stopped walking. They were on a large open space at the top of the hill, on top of which was a large gray stone statue of a saint with long robes and a veil. She was holding a cross, and her stone eyes seemed to gaze out across valley below, keeping a watchful eye on the homes and animals in all seasons. Something about her made Anna feel a moment of calm despite the jealousy that had pierced her chest just moments before.

Rose spread out a large blanket and sat down. When she opened the picnic basket, wonderful aromas spilled out. Though she offered the driver to join them, he waved his hand, thanked her and left her with the three teens and Carlotta. Rose opened the compartment in the basket that held the silverware and began to distribute forks and knives to everyone, as well as paper cups. Then she unwrapped fragrant smelling cheese and pulled fresh loaves of *baguette* out of their brown wrappers. She had filled the bread that morning with ham, butter and lettuce.

"*Miam,*" Olivia said. "*J'aime bien les sandwiches français... simples et bons* !"

Anna started. She didn't know that Olivia spoke French, nor that she knew how the French made their sandwiches. Olivia noticed her surprise.

"I had a French nanny when I was younger, and now I learn French at school," the new Royal Highness explained. "Our cook is also French."

Rose continued: "Jean-Luc used to be famous in France, what we call a *chef* étoilé – a starred chef—but he decided to move to the U.S. for a quieter life. I met him when I visited Olivia in California—what was it— six years ago already? He makes the most amazing pastries too, doesn't he, Olivia?"

"Oh yes," Olivia said, licking her lips. "He makes macarons in any color I want, whenever I want."

"Imagine if we could have a real chef for our wedding!" Rose said.

"I'll tell mom," Olivia said, reaching out for the sandwich Rose handed to her.

"It was a joke," Rose said, her hand freezing in mid-air.

"I'm sure he would say yes!" Olivia said. "He's been saying that he's needed an excuse to come back to France for a while now."

Anna sighed. Not only did Olivia look better than her today, but she spoke French better as well and was apparently well-connected. She stopped listening to the conversation and munched on her own sandwich, gazing out over the plains.

A phone ringing cut into her thoughts. It was Olivia's.

"Oh, it's mom right now!" Olivia exclaimed. "Hi mom! Sorry the reception is bad here. Can you see my friends?"

Anna bristled at the word *friends*, but she curious to see what Olivia's mother looked like and hoped to have a look into Olivia's three-pool mansion. Olivia, however, turned the phone back to herself and Anna only got a glimpse of two brown eyes peering into the camera and heard a high-pitched "Hiiiii, everyone!"

"Mom, mom, were having a picnic on a beautiful hill and we had an amazing idea!" Olivia practically squealed. "Can Jean-Luc cook for Rose's wedding? And maybe make macarons for opening day at the flower shop? You know, in lavender or rose."

"We'll see, Honey," Olivia's mom laughed. "It's not a bad idea. But I just called to remind you... since it's your last day there, why don't you reveal the big surprise?"

Olivia's eyes glittered and she bounced up and down excitedly.

"Oh, I hope she likes it!" she squealed. "Should I tell her or you, Mom?"

"Go ahead, my dear," her mother said. "Anyway, I can't hear you very well and your video keeps cutting out. Let me know what she says."

Olivia placed her phone carefully in her purse, zipped it slowly back up, then clasped her hands excitedly in front of her.

"Rose, you're my favorite cousin," Olivia said with a huge smile, and Anna watched Rose's eyebrows draw together. "We've always been like sisters. You know why."

"You're so sweet," Rose said, reaching an arm around her cousin's shoulder.

"So mom heard about... you know... the engagement party. That you cancelled it because of... um... budgeting issues."

Rose's eyes widened.

"You're not suggesting...?"

"Yes," Olivia said. "Mom and Dad want to pay for it."

Rose clasped her hands together.

"I... oh my goodness... I..."

"And Dad said it's your wedding gift anyway. From all three of us."

Rose stiffened, looked around at the others awkwardly, then smiled at her cousin and drew her into a big hug. Anna's stomach dropped as she realized that she hadn't even thought yet about what to get Rose for her wedding... or what could she offer to make Rose happy when she was currently being offered exquisite French cooking and an entire party? It all sounded ludicrous anyway. Anna jumped to her feet and walked deliberately away. Rose and Olivia, still hugging, didn't notice.

She walked around a boulder that faced the other valley. In the distance, she could just make out the highest turrets of the castle behind a cluster of houses on another hill, and the rolling forests behind it. Her anger abated somewhat. The sky was a clear blue, and its emptiness decluttered her own scrambled thoughts in her mind. She was simultaneously thinking about how Olivia was probably showing off on purpose, her angst about not looking as good as her, and that Rose didn't think of her anymore. These mixed ideas seemed to separate in her mind the longer she stared at the spacious sky, until finally they seemed, one by one, to float away on the wind into it. The last to leave was the thought of Rose, and as it did, she heard Rose calling her name a few times.

"Anna?" Rose was right behind her. "Are you ok?"

Anna felt a bit embarrassed at her flight, and also didn't want to draw attention to the fact that Olivia had just offered Rose a gift that Anna never could, and that her parents, despite their comfortable life, couldn't either.

"Yes," Anna said. "I thought I saw someone I knew over there. But they're gone."

And without looking at Rose, she returned to the blanket. She couldn't wait to go back to school. Even though she wasn't like her classmates and couldn't understand them perfectly, she at least had friends there. She was glad she wouldn't have to spend the next day at home, not knowing that another surprise, and not necessarily a nice one, would be waiting for her at school.

CHAPTER 10

Haunted

On Monday, Anna almost forgot about Olivia, as school suddenly got busy. Her History-Geography class with Monsieur Beauharnais, who was also their French teacher, was two hours long and listening to the French for so long was tiring. He was a short, balding man, with crooked wiry glasses who refused to use the computer or projector, and often went on rants about wave transmitters purposely implanted in technological devices by foreign governments or clothing brands that were ruining the planet. Even Abeni had difficulties translating certain parts of those speeches to Anna. He refused to speak English with Anna, stating that French was the most glorious language in the world, but he was not unkind to her otherwise.

He dropped the chalkboard eraser every time he was agitated, which was often, because he couldn't stand interruptions, chatting, sneezing, or students touching anything but their pens and paper, including their hair. However, he had introduced himself by stating that he didn't allow students to use erasers in the classroom, because they shouldn't make mistakes in the first place. Anna thought that Abeni had mistranslated, but it was true: when Gabin took out his eraser, it was confiscated, and Monsieur Beauharnais was so agitated that he dropped his own eraser as he threw Gabin's in the garbage.

"Cette generation qui ne prend rien au sérieux," he mumbled, and Anna and Abeni shared discreet, knowing smiles: Monsieur Beauharnais was always mumbling about their "generation".

Monsieur Beauharnais began each class by noting a list of dates and words on the blackboard in neat, round letters with different colors of chalk and spoke quite quickly. Anna felt a bit bored as she dutifully copied everything he had written about the causes of World War I. A recent movie she had seen on that time period had taught her much more about it and had been way more entertaining. He droned on a little longer, taking a few *carnets de correspondence* for everything from chatting to an "insolent look", then began to neatly print a list under the word "Devoirs". Anna knew this word well because they received a lot of it every night, even when they finished school at five: it meant "homework".

On Monday in the afternoon, Madame Marel took the class to the library. Anna was glad. Listening to French all day had made her tired. Plus, she had always loved libraries, which were good places to satisfy her curiosity and imagination, but she hadn't had many occasions to go there.

Anna smiled when she walked in. It was high-ceilinged room with hanging lamps in the shape of open, upside-down books. There were cushions and poufs and tables, too. Giant windows between some shelves stretched almost to the ceiling, and since the curtains were drawn, they lit the library in glowing sunlight. Five or so desktop computers lined the walls, and there was a cart full of tablets next to a long librarians' desk.

Anna saw a label stuck on one of the higher shelves that said *En anglais*. A whole row of books were shelved above it. *Cool!* she thought. *Books in my native language!* When Madame Marel allowed them a few minutes to explore the library on their own, the students scrambled for the computers and tablets. Anna, however, made her way to the librarian's desk.

The woman with frizzy white hair and wearing long yellow feather earrings peered down at her over thick, yellow-rimmed glasses. Her hands were folded in front of her, behind a sign that said "Madame Bouquiner", and Anna saw layers of several bracelets on each hand. The beads were small, smooth, and of a variety of colors, including pink, light blue, dark green, cream, and purple, each with wisps of white on the surface. They reminded Anna of miniature crystal balls that a fortune teller might use. The woman wore many similar rings, and Anna was amazed by the huge round turquoise rock on the librarian's ring finger. Anna tore her eyes away from the stones and grinned up at Madame Bouquiner.

"*Je veux un bon livre en anglais, s'il te plaît. J'aime l'histoire.*"

"Well!" The librarian raised her hands with joy and her many stones and beads clicked and clacked on her wrist. Anna was surprised that she spoke English. "A student who likes books. What a pleasure. But you 'ave forgotten the *vous*."

"Oops." Anna's hand flew to her mouth. She was addressing an adult and had forgotten to use the formal "vous" to say "you". She had used "te", a form of "tu", which was too familiar and used for friends and family. She flushed and then she felt a presence next to her.

"Yes, Anna, be polished," Madame Marel frowned. "You don't want to bless someone."

"She means *polite*, not *polished*," Abeni murmured from the table next to the counter. "And *hurt*, not *bless*, like the verb *blesser*."

Anna nodded, fighting back a smile.

"Je vous montre une nouveau livre en anglais," Madame Bouquiner said, easily forgetting Anna's mistake, standing up and gesturing to Anna to follow her. On the way to the English shelf, she shushed Abeni and Gabin, whose voices were rising as they talked about a video they were watching on the computer, and then stooped down under her desk.

"Voici un livre que tu vas aimer," Madame Bouquiner said, pulling herself back upright with a book in her hand.

Anna loved the cover instantly. It was a little worn, but it showed a young woman leaning on a fireplace, clutching a handful of jewelry to her heart. The necklaces spilled down the front of her long, billowing dress, and she stared protectively at the treasure held to her chest. It had a sinister but royal feel to it.

"Both history and mystery," Madame Bouquiner said.

Anna smiled gratefully. *"C'est quand qu'il faut le..."* she couldn't find the word for "hand in" so she made a gesture as if she was giving it back.

"Rendre?" Madame Bouqiner smiled. "Never. Is for you. It's not beautiful but is a beautiful gift."

Anna thanked her and sat down alone at a table to peruse the pages but didn't get far.

"'Ello, Anna." Anna looked up. Chloé and Victoria were standing over her table. They were wearing matching sweaters and pink eyeshadow. *"Tu fais quoi ?"*

"I'm reading," Anna said. *"Lire. Les livres."*

Chloé and Victoria looked at each other and giggled, then said something in French too quickly for Anna to understand. Anna didn't reply, which made Victoria giggle even more, her face reddening slightly as she tried to keep quiet. Chloé then pointed at one of the fortresses on the back cover.

"You like to live at Château Fleur?" Chloé asked.

"Oh yeah," Anna replied and couldn't help but smile. "It's like being royalty."

This was too much for Victoria, who stifled a loud laugh in her elbow.

"*Hanté*," Chloé said slowly and loudly. "You know the word, '*hanté*'"?

Of course, Anna knew the word "haunted". And why was Chloé talking to her as if she were hard of hearing?

"Château Fleur is *hanté*," Chloé smirked, pointing at the book. "You don't know it?"

"Is true," said a gentle voice behind Anna. It was Lena, padding softly around their table to get back to hers. "There is a *film*."

Chloé and Victoria giggled and flounced away to another table, where Chloe, instead of sitting down on a chair, chose the table. She crossed her legs and tossed her hair, staring at Madame Bouquiner to see when she would notice and tell her to get down. But Madame Bouquiner was busy shelving some books. Chloé gave up and began chatting with the other girls at the table.

Anna frowned. How did Chloé know where she lived? And were there really ghosts at Fleur? And why was her book making them laugh?

Her thoughts were interrupted by the sound of the library doors opening then shutting. She glanced over and couldn't believe her eyes. Madame Marel had just walked in, accompanied by none other than the New Royal Highness.

Fashion

"*Ça va pas?*" Abeni asked her as they made their way home that night.

"Nothing's wrong," Anna muttered, irritated. She tugged at the crop top underneath her sweater. Abeni had given her the shirt after Anna lied and said she liked Nella's videos—mostly just to avoid offending her new friend. She still hadn't gotten used to how short it was and hadn't dared take off her sweater at school. It seemed all wrong for an aspiring Princess.

"She's gorgeous, isn't she?" Abeni said. "I thought she was the Princess of England when she walked in!"

That's it, Anna said. *You know what's wrong.*

Olivia was wrong, all wrong. She had ruined Anna's day by coming to school. Madame Marel had brought her into the library, explaining that they had a special visitor and mistakenly telling the class that she was Anna's cousin. Then she went on to explain that Olivia was famous, was visiting France from California and that Anna had invited her to visit Sainte Madeleine occasionally to learn about French schools. Mistaken again. Anna wondered if Rose or Carlotta had set it up.

Anna couldn't help but feel like either of those two were partly responsible for ruining her day, which was already going badly thanks to the two best friends in pink eyeshadow.

"*Californie!*" Gabin exclaimed when Madame Marel had finished, his mouth open.

"Famous!" Abeni gasped, glancing at Anna.

"*Quel jolie tenue!*" Delphine exclaimed, gaping at Olivia's attire, including a pristine pink handbag that matched the pink ribbon in her hair and complimented her long, soft blue fall jacket. Her fingers were adorned with rings: small but glittery pink gems.

Even Chloé, who had been enjoying the attention from the girls at the table, looked up, astonished, but didn't move from her spot when all the girls and Victoria made their way over to Olivia.

"*Ça me fait grandement plaisir de voir votre école,*" Olivia said, dipping her head gently and flashing a large, perfectly white-toothed smile at the class. Anna couldn't see anything else after that. Her "cousin" was soon hidden behind the group that had gathered around her.

When Madame Marel's voice broke through the babble that had begun to rise and asked who would like to give her a tour of the school, several hands immediately shot up.

"And she spoke French so well," Abeni continued, and Anna was lurched back to the dirt road leading up to her home.

"Yeah," Anna answered, tugging at her shirt again and kicking at a few leaves. "Hey, look, I wore the crop top you lent me. But I covered it up so my Mom and teachers wouldn't see it." She finally pulled off her sweater. The autumn air was cool and disagreeable on the bare skin of her lower stomach. She felt strangely exposed and glanced around to make sure no one else was around, but at least her gesture had turned the conversation away from her incredible "cousin".

"It looks so good!" Abeni grinned. Anna smiled awkwardly.

CHAPTER 12

Dresses Again

Rose and Olivia began to join the dinner table at Château Fleur more and more frequently, constantly talking to Mom about the flower shop and wedding and everything Olivia's family would be doing for it and how she was such an impressive girl and how beautiful her outfits were. The only time Rose would address Anna was to ask her about a new book she had read, but it was becoming more and more rare of an occurrence. Anna would steal away early to her room to do homework.

One night, Anna left the dinner table quickly, making an excuse not to eat the cake Olivia had made them using a recipe Jean-Luc had given her (which impressed everyone, of course). Olivia would be here for an entire week, so she almost hoped that they would get enough homework at school so that she could keep to herself at night. Right now, she had to get started on her homework for Monsieur Beauharnais (explain why France would have won the war against Germany even without the United States' help) and was determined not to embarrass herself if the teacher should call on her to read her work.

"Every time you eat McDonald's, Charles de Gaulle rolls in his grave!" was the English equivalent of what he told them that day, frowning, after he announced the homework.

Anna ended up spending most of her time looking for her history workbook.

"I swear I brought it home," she said, going through her entire room. Finally, she gave up, thinking that maybe it was one of Henry's jokes, even though he hadn't stolen things from her room in years. These days, he just grabbed things right in front of her.

Mom knocked on the door around 9 p.m.

"Is everything ok?" she asked. "You didn't have much of an appetite tonight."

"Yes," Anna lied. "I have homework." As she turned around to show her paper to Mom, the book Madame Bouquiner had given her slid on to the floor.

"What is that for?" Mom asked, helping her pick them up. "They're not already reading English novels already in 3ème already, are they?"

"The librarian gave it to me. She's the nicest lady in the school, even though she doesn't speak English. And Madame Rabhi lets me read in class when I get bored."

"That's nice," Mom said in her absent-minded way. "Do you want to come up to the attic with Henry and me? I have some things I need to clear out, and I found a trunk and some boxes of your old stuff."

"Oh, you can throw it out." Anna shuddered, thinking of her old doll dress collection. "I already took the one I want to keep." *The only one that wasn't ripped to shreds*, she thought silently.

"No, no, no!" her mom said. "There are lots of interesting things in there. That parka you made last year and... and I really need more room. You have more space in your closet. Come on!"

She made for the door and Anna heaved herself up. It wouldn't hurt to look.

Carlotta led her through a series of hallways and up a few flights of stairs. She opened a pair of creaky wooden doors and Anna wandered into the low-ceilinged rooms that had probably lodged all the servants back in the day. Henry was already there, rummaging through a box with his name scrawled across the side. After interrogating him about her history book and being more or less satisfied that he wasn't the culprit, she glanced around the attic.

Not only did it contain all the boxes that Anna's family had shipped here, but one of the corners was packed with what looked like thousands of ancient books. They were piled topsy-turvy, with no apparent organization. Some were packed onto some shelves and others were in piles on the floor and the window seat, as well. There were even stacks strewn about on the rug in the middle of the room since there was no more room on the shelves. All were quite dusty, but Anna didn't mind. She reached out to inspect them. The dust made them seem older and therefore more mysterious, as if taking the book into her hands would not only tell her a good story, but also transport her to a different time period.

"Amazing, isn't it?" her mom said. "I asked the old owner if he wanted them back, but he said no. Maybe we'll clean them up and put them in the living room one day, on those big shelves."

Anna put down the centuries-old Bible she had been flipping through and took another volume that looked more contemporary. The back cover was pretty: dark green with interweaving golden flowers. She flipped it over and flinched. The front cover showed a picture of a pale, glowing white figure in a long robe standing in a stone room with a large fireplace.

Henry laughed. "Ghosts," he said.

But it wasn't the ghosts that made Anna shiver.

"Henry, look where it's standing..."

"Yeah," Henry said, not smiling anymore. "It looks like our living room!" He grabbed the book and flipped through it. It was in French.

"It's about a ghost that lives in Fleur," he said. "But it's fiction. Not real. Fleur was famous back in the day. Well, it still is. There are lots of books about it. A movie was even filmed here once. What was it called again?"

Anna grabbed the book back from him and placed it back on the shelf. She didn't care if the book was fiction. After what Chloé had told her, and because her books had mysteriously gone missing today, she didn't want to think about ghosts anymore.

"Oh right, it was called *Château Haunted*," Henry said thoughtfully.

Anna stared at him. "Stop, not funny."

"It was! But it was fiction. And a flop, I heard." He shrugged and went back to his box. Anna's stomach clenched up, but she decided to put it out of her mind. *Henry was right,* she told herself. *Just fiction.*

Her mom helped her haul her boxes and a trunk back to her room.

"See? They'll fit in your closet!" her mom said before leaving her alone for the rest of the night.

Anna stared at the trunk. There they were, the dresses, strewn across the top, exactly as Anna had left them in anger when they had been ruined. She blushed as she thought about the incident at her old school, but she also realized she had missed them. She pulled some of them to the side and found her old sewing machine at the bottom.

Then she remembered what Rose had said about her "doll dresses." Suddenly, Anna had a revelation.

A wedding gift, she thought. *Handmade. Flowers. Just the sort of thing Rose likes!*

"Lilith isn't here anyway," she decided, and pulled out her second-favorite doll dress: A black one with the long train of red roses. All she had to do was make it bigger. At human size, it would be magnificent, and it was her last chance to show Rose that her Little American still existed. She had the skill to make something meaningful, even if it turned out less beautiful than anything Olivia could buy.

"It's not beautiful, but a beautiful gift."

She was proud of her project, and was sure that in the end, she would outdo—or at least match—Rose's perfect cousin.

CHAPTER 13

Almost Friends

More and more autumn leaves began to coat the countryside with orange, yellow, brown and red hues, and the air was getting colder and colder. Anna enjoyed her morning walks to school. Abeni joined her halfway to school every morning and, as they crunched through frosted leaves on the cobblestones streets that led through the center, Abeni updated her on Nellas's latest videos.

Anna pretended to be interested: She didn't want to lose her best friend, especially with the competition from Olivia. But her mind wandered to the last few weekends working tirelessly on the Rose dress. With each flower she finished or each dainty pearl she attached, she became more and more confident in her skill, and secretly glad that she could do something different from her classmates, who seemed to just scroll through Nella videos.

Plus, she had other reasons to feel more optimistic. Her classes were going quite well. Her French was improving quickly, and she had even gotten good grades on most of her exams, except in French class where Monsieur Beauharnais didn't seem to make any exception for the fact that French was not her native language and even refused to translate instructions for her. She did her best, and studied her spelling and grammar every night, hoping to show the stern French teacher that she could do almost as well as a French student.

One day, she was even surprised when Chloé, followed by Victoria, who had been strangely kind to her all day, came over to her in the courtyard between classes.

"*Tu m'aides*? Help?" Chloé said, pointing to her English workbook. Anna was taken aback. She still felt slightly annoyed about the library incident. Chloé seemed to read her mind.

"Sorry for the library," Chloé said. "It was just a *blague*."

Anna wasn't sure if it had just been a *joke*, but then a thought occurred to her.

Maybe if I help Chloé with her homework, the teasing would stop.

"*Pararaphe*," Chloé said. "*Tu m'aide à l'écrire?* Help write?"

Madame Rabhi had assigned a small paragraph to write. They had to describe the superheroes they had been studying: their superpowers, their clothes, the villains they fought. It had of course been easy for Anna.

Chloé sat down on one side, placing her purse by her side. It was one of those shiny, leather ones like Olivia's and had Chloé's name printed on it. Victoria sat on Anna's other side, brushing off her shiny, bright white sneakers with bright orange streaks. She always had new shoes, Anna noticed.

Anna began pointing to the superheroes on Chloé's worksheet and giving the Chloé the words to describe them. Chloé began writing, then sighed.

"*Ça va prendre trop de temps comme* ça," she said, pointing to her watch. "No time. I copy?" She pointed to Anna's book.

Anna was surprised but flipped open her book and let Chloé copy her paragraph. When Chloé was finished, she shut the book and pulled her purse onto her lap to tuck her notebook inside.

"*Tu n'as pas de sac à main?*" Chloé asked Anna. "You no have bag?"

"Oh no," Anna said, embarrassed, glancing at her backpack. Most girls got rid of their backpack after one or two years of middle school and replaced it with a large handbag for both books and personal items.

"My purse is too small. I'm getting a bigger one for Christmas. *Pour Noel!*"

Chloé smirked and stood up and Victoria did the same.

"*Elle est en 3ème et elle n'a pas de sac à main!*" They laughed and left. Anna felt her face getting warm in both anger and embarrassment, but before she had time to run after Chloé and demand at least a "thank you" for the homework help, the music on the loudspeaker signaled the end of the *récré*, or recess. Anna shuffled over to her class's line and moved in next to Abeni, then followed the group up the stairs to English class.

"Please take out your homework," Mrs. Rabhi said slowly after they had finished their warm-up exercises. "I will choose five students to read."

She spun the little name wheel and it landed on Gabin first. He read his paragraph to which Mrs. Rabhi could simply nod, wide-eyed, pretending to understand his impossible accent but too kind to say anything about it.

"Chloé!" Mrs. Rabhi had spun the wheel one last time, and when she announced the name of the lucky student, Anna was pulled from her daydreaming.

Chloé stood up, smiled and fluttered her eyes at Mrs. Rabhi, threw her shoulders back and lifted her notebook. She proudly read out the paragraph, mispronouncing a few words. Then she smiled again at the teacher and sat down.

"Marvelous!" Mrs. Rabhi said. "Did you have help on that? An online translator?"

"No help," Chloé said. *"J'ai cherché pleins de mots en ligne et j'ai bien révisé la grammaire que vous nous aviez donné !"*

"You looked up a lot of words online," Mrs. Rabhi smiled. "And yes, I can see that you studied the grammar and applied it. Well done!"

Anna's stomach turned and she stared at Chloé, who sat down and smirked at Anna. Mrs. Rabhi didn't notice, which made Anna even angrier. She turned red and stared straight ahead. How dare Chloé steal her work, make fun of her for not having a handbag, and then pass the paragraph off as her own! Anna didn't dare say anything, though. All the teachers seemed to like Chloé, and she didn't want things to get worse. She bit her lip and pulled out a piece of paper for the vocabulary quiz, placing her divider firmly in place so that Chloé couldn't see it from across the aisle. She was glad to be on vacation at the end of the week.

CHAPTER 14

Doubts

Olivia came back to Saint Madeleine to sit in on a few classes and be the center of attention. Anna could feel that her classmates' enthusiasm for herself was not as intense as it had been. Just a few weeks ago, Gabin, Delphine and the others would have stared admiratively at Anna every time she spoke English. But these days, Gabin's attention had wandered to the ceiling as it often did in Mrs. Rabhi's class, and he occasionally made a dreamy comment about how cool California must be. Though far from being in love with him, Anna felt a stab of jealousy for what she suspected was Gabin's crush on Olivia.

Even Delphine seemed to be moving on. Today she was letting Chloé draw little pictures on her pencil case with a neon marker and not paying attention at all when Miss Rabhi did her usual example conversation with Anna. Inès just looked straight-up bored, and Abeni was secretly studying her science notes under her English book. And at recess the day before, she had seen Lena scrolling through Olivia's social media feed with her friends and saying something about how Olivia was coming to her party.

Anna was relieved when the bell rang and history class began, especially since Olivia was sitting this one out, but only for a moment. She wasn't thrilled when Monsieur Beauharnais chose her to read out her homework assignment, a long essay on how history was important in their daily lives, which he had given the class because he "did not detect enough academic enthusiasm for history" in his class.

Luckily, Anna had found the missing history workbook to help her with the assignment. The book turned up one night when she almost slipped on it in the hallway near the bathroom. She still hadn't solved the mystery of how it had gotten there.

Anna stood up and read her paragraph, which she had carefully corrected online.

"Some of my hobbies are directly related to history. I read historical books and love the fashion in them," she paused. She had hesitated about the next part, but Rose's conversation this summer had convinced her to be proud of her unique hobby. "In middle school, I liked to sew, so I made a collection of Victorian dresses for a contest at school. Small ones, that could be used for 18-inch dolls, but ..."

Chloé snorted aloud, and Victoria stifled a giggle.

"*Chloé* !" Monsieur exclaimed. "*Explique-moi pourquoi tu rigoles ! Toute de suite*!"

Chloé stopped laughing and she smiled sweetly at the teacher.

"*C'est juste... Monsieur...*" – Victoria began to giggle for real this time, then stopped and put on a serious face- "*Elle a joué avec des poupets quand elle était au college* "

This time, a few other students joined in the giggling, but with a stern look from the teacher, they stopped. Monseiur Beauharnais frowned and dropped the eraser again, said something else, then beckoned to Anna.

"Zank you, Anna," he said in heavily accented English, the first time Anna had heard him speaking her language. She thought she also detected a bit of pity in his voice, which wasn't very characteristic of him. "You sit down. And ze next time you write essay for zis class, you speak about France, not ze Queen Victoria, ok?"

"What exactly did Chloé say?" Anna whispered to Abeni as slid quickly back into her chair, not sure she had understood everything. Abeni shook her head.

"Nothing," she replied. "It's not important."

Abeni didn't talk to Anna for the rest of the hour, but when the bell rang and they gathered their things, Anna followed Abeni into the hallway.

"Abeni," she insisted. "What does *"joué avec des poupets"* mean? I think that's what I understood."

"Oh, it means 'play with dolls,'" Abeni said. "You know, like little children do."

Anna blushed and stared at her feet.

"They weren't really *for* the dolls!" Anna said. "It was a school assignment. And I was like, twelve years old."

Abeni cocked her head at Anna, not sure what to say. After a moment, she said, "Monsieur Beauharnais told Chloé you're American, and your country is full of strange traditions, so maybe that's why. I mean, I don't care. But Chloé and Victoria are strange sometimes, like I said. Anyway, I gotta go to the Vie Scolaire and see why I was marked absent yesterday. *A bientôt!*"

"See you soon," Anna replied. She felt a little ashamed and annoyed as she watched Abeni walk off. She hoped that Abeni was just in a bad mood and not taking Chloé's side. Maybe Monsieur Beauharnais was right. She wasn't like the other students, with her different language and culture, so she would have to be extra careful about what she said in class in the future. Especially if Chloé was there.

No one's impressed with my English anymore, she thought. *They were way more impressed with Olivia... and now Chloé. And I need to forget about the dress. Maybe Rose was just being nice and thinks it's stupid, too.*

She swallowed a lump in her throat and made her way to the technology classroom on the other side of the courtyard. Olivia was already there, surrounded by an admiring group, showing her necklace to Delphine. Anna wondered if her own life was still the fairy tale Delphine had once thought it was.

CHAPTER 15

Plans

To her relief, Abeni still waited for her at the gate and came over for *apéro* as she had started doing almost every Friday night. Apéro was Carlotta's latest French craze. Pre-dinner snacks of chips, sausage and cheese, normally with wine. But since her latest health care banned alcohol, and the kids were too young, she would make them herbal cocktails instead. Anna had already pointed out that vast amounts of cheese and sausage probably weren't good for a detox diet, but her Mom pretended not to hear her.

Another surprise was awaiting her, too.

"Report cards!" Henri said, gesturing to the table.

"Check my grades, Mom," he said, holding out the envelope. "I only got written up three times. Can I have my phone back now?"

"Well, it's getting better," Mom sighed. "But you'll be working during *Vacances de la Toussaint.*"

Anna flinched at her mom's awkward pronunciation of All Saint's vacation, a two-week fall break. Abeni hid a smile behind her cocktail.

"Bleh," Henry said, holding out an envelope to his sister. "Let's see, Highness. Anything below an A? I mean, a twenty?"

She ignored his mocking tone, glad he was using her nickname for her again. She tore open the envelope and scanned down the list. Her first report card, or *bulletin de notes*, came out at the end of the month, and Mom was more than pleased. Her teachers had written nice comments, even Monsieur Beauharnais, who noted her efforts and progress in French class, though she had only received an eight. Anna had learned that in French middle schools, under ten was not usually a good grade and was the equivalent of a D or F in the American system. A twenty was considered perfect but was hard to achieve. She had a twenty in English class though, and it balanced out the French grade. Overall, she received a *mention*, or honors, called *compliments*, meaning her average was over thirteen. Only her grade in French prevented her from receiving the highest honors, called *félicitations*, and she made it her goal for the end of the year.

"Nice," Abeni said. "Nothing below 10 except in French. Like everyone else."

"What are you doing for vacation, Abeni?" Mom asked, passing around a plate of hard *comté* cheese.

"Nothing," Abeni said. "We're staying here and family is visiting."

"Too bad Mom is so strict," Henry said. "I would have invited you two to all the parties the high schoolers are having this week. I even talked Matthis into inviting Olivia."

"Home by 11," Carlotta muttered and Henry pretended not to hear.

"Olivia!" Anna exclaimed suddenly, realizing what Henry had said, and her stomach dropped. "She'll be here during vacation?"

"I wanted to have her over tonight," Mom said. "She was here this afternoon with Rose but they went to the city to get measurements for wedding outfits. I'm sorry, Anna."

Anna nodded stiffly.

"She has to travel a lot for her concerts and for her mom's job," Henry said, reiterating what Anna already knew, of course. "She's so cool. She said she has a movie theater in her house. Mom, we should do that here, but like a gaming arena instead of showing movies!"

Mom raised her eyebrows.

"Yeah, she's like a legend at school," Abeni chimed in. "It's the only famous person we've ever met here."

Anna stared straight ahead and tried to think hard of something else.

"I just hope we can celebrate Halloween," Henry was saying when she returned to the conversation. "I don't know if we do that here. I'll ask Matthis."

"Do they trick-or-treat here?" Anna asked.

Henry and Abeni looked at her strangely.

"Trick-or-treat?" her brother laughed. "How old are you, five?"

"I was just wondering," Anna said, then had an idea: she could save face in front of her brother and Abeni, and also show her classmates that she was as cool as Olivia and Matthis.

"I want to have a party this year," Anna said, sitting up straight and looking her mom in the eyes. "Here. With Abeni and Gabin and some kids from my class. It will better than Matthis's," she added, wagging her head at Henry.

"Doubtful," he whispered back. "And Olivia will be with us."

"Alright," Mom shrugged, not hearing Henry. "But the 11 o'clock rule still applies here."

"See," Henri smirked, but Anna didn't care, because Abeni's eyes were glowing.

"Yes, my first real Halloween!" Abeni exclaimed. She pulled out her phone. "Let's make notes. What do we need?"

Anna rolled up sleeves and scooted up closer to the table. Her heart felt lighter in her chest. Abeni was definitely on her side again.

CHAPTER 16

Noises

Everything was in place. The projector for the scary movie, a fire in the fireplace, pumpkins they had found at the open-air market, knives to slice faces on, piles of the American snacks that Mom had rush ordered from Paris, and the eyeball gummies floating in punch. Carlotta and Jake had promised to stay well out of the way. Her mom had offered to watch Pamplemousse while Olivia was off at her party and Rose away visiting relatives, so that would keep her busy. The last thing Anna needed was for her classmates to have her strange American parents hovering around.

Gabin was the first to arrive with his friend Brleg. When Gabin tripped into the living room (Anna realized he never walked more than a few feet without some sort of stumble), his eyes doubled in size.

"Whoah, I'm in the USA!" he said, and grabbed a knife.

"Let's wait for the others," Abeni said, gently taking it back. "Don't leave him alone with the knives," she whispered to Anna, who laughed.

When everyone else was there—Delphine, Inès, Lena, and her friend Marie—they got to work, babbling in a mix of French and English and mostly understanding each other. When they were done, they placed them all over the living room with candles inside, which they would light when it got dark. Gabin hadn't taken the time to trace the eyes, nose and mouth before cutting them out, so the whole face was lopsided, but he was pleased.

"Woooaaahhh," Inès exclaimed as the jack-o-lanterns were lit. They glowed against the dark window. The fireplace flickered through the room, casting shadows along the walls. "This is a real 'alloween *ambience*, like in ze American movies."

Then Anna showed them how to roast pumpkin seeds in the oven.

"Ew," Brieg said, crunching down a few. "*Pas super.* But I feel like a cool American!"

Anna's heart was lifting even more.

Later they settled into the chairs and poufs for a movie.

"*Ghosts of Halloween Past*?" Abeni frowned.

"Boring," Brieg said. "How about something actually scary? I haven't seen *The Duke* yet. It's about a ghost with a saw who comes out of the fireplaces in a castle. Did you know that the original was made here?"

Anna shivered. Another portrayal of her home? She had a bad feeling about it. But everyone was nodding their heads, and she didn't want them to report back to her other classmates that she was, indeed, a child.

"Yeah and Delphine has experience with this!" Abeni laughed.

Delphine shook her head.

"It's just a legend," she said. "There was a duke in my family who lived here a long time ago. My great-great-great... great grandfather? I don't remember exactly the story but apparently a ghost murdered him while trying to steal a precious manuscript. A ghost that came out of the fireplace. It inspired the movie, but not exactly."

"Here?" Anna exclaimed, hardly able to conceal her shiver. "At Fleur?"

"It's just a story," Abeni said, looking at her incredulously. Anna swallowed and straightened up.

"Yeah, of course," she said as confidently as she could. She glanced at Brieg, who was looking for the movie on her laptop. The movie's icon didn't look so bad: just a fireplace with the vague shadow of a duke in front of it.

She closed her eyes through much of the first part. Though it hadn't been filmed at Fleur, it still felt too close to home.

Suddenly, just as the ghost on screen had plunged the knife into the duke's neck... *boom*! There was a noise that sounded like it was coming from the wall with the window or the ceiling above it. Everyone jumped. Lena screamed. Gabin knocked over his glass of punch. Brieg ran to the window while Anna's entire body seemed to have turned to stone. He turned around.

"There's no one there," he said, making his way back to the couch. "Maybe upstairs?"

Another *thump*. This time, everyone yelled and ran to the window, except Anna, still frozen in her seat.

"No one!" Abeni cried.

Then Brieg began to laugh. Inès, too. Soon they were all giggling. `

"*Trop bien!*" Delphine said. "Did you see Anna's face?"

"Relax, Anna," Abeni said, coming back. "It's just a tree branch or something."

Anna was still frozen but forced out a laugh.

When everyone had left, Anna started to clean up the living room, as she had promised her mom. As she extinguished the fire in the fireplace and blew out the last jack-o-lantern candle, another noise made her flinch so violently that she almost knocked the pumpkin over.

"Oh sorry," Olivia called out from the doorway. She was wearing a magnificent shiny black dress and the black makeup on her face was smeared. Henry was standing behind her. "Oooo what nice decorations!"

She moved into the room.

"I'll leave you here," Henry said, and Anna was horrified to see him smile a large, goofy grin, raise the mask in his hand gently in an awkard "goodbye" motion, and move towards the stairs, his eyes still on the girl from California. Was her brother... *being a gentleman*? Had he *walked her home*? Why was her *makeup smeared*? Was he *in love* with Olivia?

"Did you make those?" Olivia asked, gesturing to the jack o' lanterns, oblivious to the tone in which she had just been addressed.

"My friends did. We had a party here tonight." She checked to make sure all the flames had been extinguished. "They loved it," she added deliberately.

"Nice!" Olivia said, and it annoyed Anna that she sounded sincere.

"How was Matthis's party?"

"Oh great," Olivia said. "But you know, I'm not much for parties. I prefer a quiet night by the fire. You have a magnificent one here." She pointed to the embers across the room. Anna was annoyed that she secretly agreed with everything Olivia had just said. Olivia finally seemed to notice the tension.

"Oh, don't worry about Henry," she said shaking her head. "I think he has a little thing for me, but I'm not interested." Anna didn't say anything, so she hastily added, "I mean, your brother is sweet, but I sort of already have a crush in California."

"Yeah," Anna said. "No worries."

"Well," Olivia said after an awkward pause. "I'll go up. Carlotta gave me the room at the end of the ballroom for the night. It's magnificent. The ballroom, I mean." She smiled that annoyingly genuine smile. "See you then!"

As soon as she left, Anna realized that she was very alone in the living room. She made for her bedroom as soon as possible, wanting to be safe in her canopy bed.

CHAPTER 17

Still Friends

In December, the orange and brown leaves falling softly around Fleur occasionally transformed into small white crystals that blanketed the land and trees on the property. Anna was glad to watch them glitter and twinkle in the afternoon sun and under the moonlight. It made living in a supposedly haunted castle seem less dramatic.

"Anna, I hear you have a dumb Halloween party," Chloé whispered as walked past to her desk one afternoon.

Anne pretended not to understand.

"They told me you were shaking because of the ghhoooooosts," she said in French. Anna said nothing. She watched Delphine doodling with Chloé on her pencil case again and realized that Delphine was probably the culprit.

"I shouldn't have invited her to Halloween," she thought. "She's known Chloé for longer than she's known me. She'll always be on Chloé's side."

One day, as Monsieur Beauharnais prattled away in his rapid French, Anna lost her concentration and stared out the window, gazing away over the rolling fields dusted with patches of snow. Turning back, Chloé caught her eye, then whispered something to Victoria.

"*Je note vos devoirs,*" Monsieur Beauharnais was saying and turned to the chalkboard to scribble the instructions for their project, which was due before Christmas break in a few weeks. As the students copied it in their *agendas*, a pen clattered behind him near his heels. He whirled around.

"*C'était qui?*" he asked, glaring at the students. No one moved. Then Victoria and Chloé glanced at Anna simultaneously and purposefully so that the teacher would notice. He stared at Anna.

"*C'était toi?*" he asked.

Anna opened her mouth, but the French words didn't come. She glanced at Chloé, who narrowed her eyes in a threatening way, and suddenly she felt a touch of fear—how was she supposed to explain this in French? Anna looked down at her agenda.

"*Le carnet de correspondence,*" Mr. Beauharnais barked, and Anna, her face feeling intensely hot, pulled it out from her bag. Her stomach turned over as she handed it to him. The song signaling the end of her school day played over the loudspeakers as he dismissed the class while filling out her little book, which she knew Mom had to sign too. She felt her face redden even more at the thought. Her Mom had been so happy with her last report card, and Anna was embarrassed to have her sign the booklet like a child.

When the last students had filed out, Mr. Beauharnais finished his signature and handed the *carnet* back to Anna, saying something about how surprised he was at her behavior. She finally found her voice.

"C'était Chloé," she said.

Mr. Beauharnais's eyes widened, then narrowed.

"Chloé ?" he said. *"Elle ne fais jamais des choses comme ça !"*

"I promise," she said desperately. *"Promesse."*

Mr. Beauharnais shook his head. *"Vous voulez que j'ajoute une remarque pour mensonge ?"*

He was threatening to write her up again, this time for lying. Horrified at the idea of getting not one but two remarks in her *carnet de correspondence*, and once again losing her ability to speak French, she said nothing more, took back her little book and fled the room, almost bumping into Abeni, who, she realized, had been listening at the door. Tears of rage welled up as she practically ran through the hallway, unsure of where she was going, and just trying to put as much distance as possible between her and the teacher and the school in general. She didn't want to be at this Saint Madaleine anymore, or anything associated with it, not even Abeni. As she made her way home, she thought about how it was almost tempting to get back to Lillith and Crew, where at least she wouldn't have to have all of her classes with the same people, day after day.

When Anna got back to her room, she went to her closet. She pulled out the Rose dress. It was the only thing she felt like doing. A few hours of focusing intensely on attaching a few more petals to the train would make her forget Chloé. It would also put off showing her *carnet de correspondence* to her mother for a signature, or doing homework, which would remind her of school. She pushed aside her sewing box and reached to the back of the closet for the dress, but her fingers lingered in the air before stretching back further to... the wall.

Where is it? she muttered, rummaging around in the closet. *Maybe I left it on my desk.*

She went over to her work area and rummaged around some more, but before she could find the dress, she was distracted by something beyond the window at the gate. It was Abeni, waving her phone in the air. Anna picked up hers and saw that she had missed four messages from her friend.

"Couldn't catch up to you," one read. Then, "I went back to Monsieur Beauharnais and told him what happened. I'm the délégué de classe, so he believes me."

The next one said, "No worries. Don't sign the *carnet* and you can talk to him on Friday."

And finally, "Already late, gotta go."

Anna sent a heart to her friend and waved in gratitude out the window, which was starting to cloud over in the approaching winter weather. She sighed in relief. Abeni was still on her side. She seemed to still have one loyal friend. Her crown had been broken for a while, but it wasn't shattered yet. She went back to looking for the Rose dress.

CHAPTER 18

A Concert

Christmas vacation came quickly, and Fleur was now surrounded by fields of snow. Anna could have stayed for hours at the window, enjoying the light snowfall, gazing out across the grounds and the fields beyond the fence. Just yesterday she had done so while debating whether to get her homework out of the way or wait until the last day of vacation. She finally decided that the Rose dress was more important. It had been missing for two days and she was beginning to panic. Luckily, the dress was eventually found in the living room, strewn under a coffee table in front of the fireplace. Anna had turned over several theories about how it had gotten there, and interrogated all family members, but the disappearance would remain a mystery. She tried not to think about the link between missing objects, the fireplace and what she had learned about Fleur at Halloween.

What was important was that the dress was back, and she could alternate between sewing, messaging Abeni who was visiting relatives overseas, and staring out the window. School might not always be easy, she decided, but France was beautiful. She had seen lots of postcard-worthy winter displays ever since the snow had arrived: a team of large workhorses dashing through the road leading to the vineyards, pulling a seemingly handmade wooden sleigh, creaking loudly under the weight of a large-bellied man and his smaller version at his side. Today, however, the large black SUV rolling to a stop just under her window had quite the opposite effect of the light swish of tails and manes in the cold winter air.

The driver's door opened; and in a quick, confident movement, the driver got out and turned around to open Olivia's door. The girl turned and sat on the edge of the seat for a moment, looking around in wonder at the snow. She was wearing shiny red ankle boots, white leggings, and a white-and-red plaid dress under a red winter coat. Anna marveled at the thick black fur surrounding her wrists and neck and large black fur hat with a bright red flower just above Olivia's ear. Her shiny red gloves matched her boots and clutched the chain of a large black handbag with fur that matched the coat and hat. Her driver pulled out an umbrella seemingly from thin air and walked her to the side of the castle.

Anna glanced down at the outfit she had chosen for dinner. Knowing Olivia would be coming, she had once again tried to dress up a little. She had carefully chosen the prettiest dress she could find at the store last week with Mom, and the prettiest sweater to wear over it, but now, next to Olivia, it seemed as if she had made no effort at all. Anna sighed sharply, took her time brushing her hair and adding a few pieces of jewelry to her outfit, and then watched a few more videos from Abeni, hoping to kill some more time so that she wouldn't have to spend too much with Olivia. An hour later, Mom called her downstairs.

Olivia was seated in front of the living room fireplace on a chair facing Rose. Mom was on the loveseat and Henry on his tablet on the floor. His good grades had earned him the right to an hour of fun screen time per day. She had taken off her coat but had kept her hat, and her hands were wrapped around a mug of hot chocolate.

"I just love real fireplaces," she was telling Mom as the flames danced before her. "Dad installed a big electric one in the living room, but it doesn't have the same smell."

Mom smiled the way she always did when Olivia spoke to her, as if she was impressed.

"I'm glad you like it," Mom said. "I also love your hat, even though I don't think animals should be killed for their fur..."

"No worries," Olivia replied. "It's synthetic but looks and feels exactly like real fur. Mom found them when we were in Sweden."

"Wonderful!" Mom exclaimed, and Rose nodded enthusiastically in agreement. Even Henry looked up from his tablet, his eyes a little too puppy-like for Anna's liking.

Anna crept back out of the room and made for the den, plopping heavily down into her favorite armchair. Her body plunking down into the chair brought her to another realization: Even sitting down, Olivia seemed to float, carrying herself in a graceful, gentle way that reflected the fluid, neat seems of her brand-name dress and the smoothness of her shiny boots. The way she waved her hands gently as she spoke bounced the light of her rings and bracelets across the shine of her handbag. Anna fought to convince herself that this was probably all an act, but it was difficult. Olivia was such a natural at all of it.

Abeni was a natural at wearing her sporty, modern fashion, too, Anna realized. *Yet I don't feel angry at her for it*, she thought.

And then she ruminated on the idea that being in Olivia's presence wasn't just about her clothes and her natural grace in them: it was also that Olivia made her feel insignificant and ignored. The rich visitor from America was talented, well-spoken, bilingual and, most importantly, captivated the heart of someone Anna admired: Rose. She thought of the dresses she was making, wondering how she could make her gift even better, when a knock at the doorway jolted her back to the den.

Henry poked in his head.

"Stop being anti-social," Henry said.

"I'm not anti-social," Anna said.

"Anti-social means you ignore everyone and pout in your armchair," he grinned. "So yeah, you are."

"Sometimes people like being alone, Henry," she said. "And thinking. You know, using your brain."

Henry smirked. "Oh good, you're getting better at comebacks. You used to just throw stuff at me. Anyway, we're gonna play *tarot* before dinner." He saw the look on her face and continued, "*Tarot* is a card game old French people play. It's kind of boring but Dad likes it. There's always a prize, and I know how to cheat so I always win. You can play with me."

Anna was intrigued by the large, vintage-looking playing cards he held up, and glad to spend time with the entire family together, her parents having put aside their many hobbies for one evening, at least. Then another unpleasant thought came to mind.

"Is Olivia playing?"

When Henry nodded, Anna stood up. She liked the idea of winning at something against Olivia. They went down to the dining room where the game was set out. Mom was finishing lighting up the fireplace and snow was falling outside the frosted window. Rose and Olivia were sitting on one end of the table and Dad on the other, dealing out large cards. Anna sat down with Henry and saw that the cards were a bit old and faded. Though they looked like a normal deck of playing cards with kings, queens, jacks and the like, they had pictures of minstrels, soldiers, farmers, and other images from far in the past that didn't resemble a traditional deck at all.

"A game I learned over at old Jacques's," Dad announced. "I'm a regular guest at his Friday evening *apéros* now."

"I'll just watch," Olivia said. "My mom is messaging me and it's hard to concentrate on both at once." She bowed her head to her phone, and the others began to play. Dad began dealing the cards and explaining the rules about bidding on the card called the *chien*.

"*Chien*?" Anna asked.

"Yes, the dog," Dad smiled. He continued to talk about how to play rounds, or tricks, and then earn points for each trick played. Anna was a little lost in his long explanations but after being guided through a round or two with Henry, she understood a little better.

After a few rounds, Olivia had placed her phone back in her sack and leaned forward on the table, her chin cupped in her hands. She caught Anna's eye, who looked away, but when Anna looked back a few moments later, Olivia's eyes had a faraway look and slowly drifted from the fireplace to the piano.

"Can I?" she asked Mom, who nodded without looking up, concentrating on her next play. Anna watched as the beautiful girl from California floated over to the grand piano, swished aside her skirt with a delicate motion, and sat down on the black leather bench. She raised her hands in a graceful, fluid motion, like a ballerina, and closed her eyes. She breathed in slowly and as her chest fell, she opened her eyes and lay her fingers delicately on the keyboard. Anna couldn't look away. She was spellbound by the gentle movements and was waiting eagerly to see which sounds Olivia could make the piano produce.

As Olivia's fingers gently pressed the keys, hovered for a few seconds, then proceeded to touch a few more, sweet music floated across the room. It was a gentle song, slow but not unhappy, that matched the pianist's movements and the whisps of snow that were blowing across the windowpane outside. Even the flames in their quicker movements seemed to die down at the sound of the instrument to match its pace. The whole room and even the weather outside seemed to succumb to the warm, gentle atmosphere that floated from the piano and its player.

When Anna did manage to look away for a second, she realized that she was not the only one in a trance. Mom, Dad and Henry were staring at Olivia in rapt attention, their game forgotten. Rose had placed her cards down before her, not caring that everyone around her could have seen them if they had been able to tear their eyes away from the show.

Olivia continued, her eyes flicking up from time to time to her audience, her smile becoming broader as she saw how much they appreciated it. The pace quickened, matching the beat of Anna's heart. She didn't like that the others were once again amazed by Olivia's presence; and she didn't like that she too liked the music.

The music, like the snow outside the castle and the fire within, became louder and quicker until Olivia's fingers were flying left and right, her eyes once again closed, her entire body moving with the music. Finally, the last five notes, powerful and drawn out, announced the end of the song, and her audience burst into applause.

Anna didn't move. Her eyes were wide. She was impressed, and in awe, but she uncomfortable with the feeling. When Dad leaned over to Mom and murmured, "She's outstanding," Anna felt her stomach sink. Dad had never said that about her before. The only talent she did have—sewing—had usually just been met with a "Huh, nice" on his part.

"It's your turn," Anna said to Henry, pointing to his cards and trying to tear her family's attention away from the talented pianist. No one seemed to hear her, least of all Henry.

"Keep going, Olivia," Mom said kindly. "I could listen to that all evening!"

"It's amazing, isn't it?" Rose said, smiling proudly at her cousin. Olivia smiled shyly, and Anna even thought her cheeks had reddened a bit, but she continued to play. After two more songs, their game of tarot had been completely forgotten, and everyone had put down their cards like Rose had and turned their chairs towards the piano. Everyone except Anna. She stared sadly into the fireplace, feeling even sadder as she realized that nobody had noticed that she was unhappy at this moment. She wished she were at school, where even if Chloé and Victoria were annoying, she still had a friend.

A Winter Event

The engagement party provided by Olivia and her family was magnificent, of course, and took place the week before Christmas.

It took place in the large dining room behind the smaller one in which they usually ate meals. Anna loved its high ceiling and wooden walls carved with animals, grapevines and different types of flowers. The tall windows along the walls were now completely frosted in the cold winter air, but when Anna rubbed her sleeve across a patch, she could see that new snowflakes were falling across the grounds. There was a large fireplace that Carlotta had lit up high for the occasion, and Anna was seated close to it and its cozy warm glow.

Rose was there with her fiancé, of course, and his three siblings, plus cousins, aunts and uncles. Rose's mother had flown in from the US where she had been visiting family. In France, the maid and man of honor were called *témoin*—witnesses—and were Rose's best friend from Paris and her fiancé's cousin. Mom, Dad and Henry were seated on Anna's left, and Henry was talking to Olivia on the other side of the thick oak table, asking her with wide eyes about a Korean celebrity who had posted a video of her playing the piano in Seoul.

Anna tried to look anywhere but at Rose's pretty, accomplished cousin. She marveled at the ceilings, which had been strung with holly and ivy. A large Christmas tree stretching up to the ceiling decorated one corner, and it was so packed with glittering silver and red ornaments and garland that Anna could hardly make out the branches underneath. A red crystal star sat atop it, glinting in many different shades, flickering with the light of the fire. A grand piano stood in the corner decked with shiny white garland. Candles had been placed in the windows. They weren't real but the wicks danced back and forth, making the tiny flames look real. There was even a snow machine that looked like a giant waterfall. Instead of water, snowflakes cascaded over the top.

Anna suddenly remembered that it had been Olivia's family who had planned and paid for all of this. It made her like it all a little less. They had even paid for the delicious food. They feasted on foie gras; *coquilles Saint-Jacques*, or scallops; and large platters of hard and soft cheeses on warm bread. Anna was disappointed that she liked it so much, and felt ashamed at the seemingly simple Halloween party she had hosted. She knew she should be happy for Rose, whose smile was radiant and whose eyes glittered with enthusiasm as they listened in admiration to Olivia's explanations, but she felt instead that usual feeling of inferiority.

"If you ever get tired of the piano," Mom said to Olivia. "You should go into the wedding business. You're already great at planning events!"

"Speaking of piano," Rose's friend chimed in. "We've all heard that you're excellent. I would like to hear it!"

Olivia blushed but smiled sweetly, and when Rose nodded at her, she took her place behind the piano once again. Anna squeezed her eyes shut to avoid rolling them in annoyance.

"Go ahead, my Little American," Rose called out, and Anna froze when she heard Rose using her nickname for someone else.

Anna's shock eventually melted into boredom. She stayed for dessert (but only because the coconut-covered cupcakes and shiny silver macarons were irresistible), then left as quickly as she could. She headed to the stairs, pausing in front of the fireplace before exiting the room. Why was the Rose dress on the floor again, just inches from the dying embers? She glanced around. No one was watching, and no one seemed to have noticed it. Anna picked it up, grasped it to her chest, heaved a few heavy breaths, then fled to her room as quickly as possible to avoid seeing any phantoms along the way.

CHAPTER 20

Return of the Ghost

Anna didn't mind that Christmas vacation had ended. Even though she had been thrilled with her Christmas presents—Mom and Dad had gotten her the prettiest blue purse that could almost rival Olivia's—Olivia was gone, which heightened her mood. At school, Monsieur Beauharnais was back to confiscating items from Gabin, including a pen that "made too much noise" when he wrote and his gym shorts that were poking out of his backpack on the floor, posing "a tripping hazard for the teacher" (even though Monsieur Beauharnais never walked through the aisles).

In fact, with Anna's French improving every day and Abeni's occasional help, French class was going more smoothly. In fact, all of Anna's conversations with everyone seemed to be easier: whether they spoke in

French or in English, it was easier to understand each other's mistakes when they shared both languages. With Madame Marel in math class, however, quite the opposite was happening.

"*Va nettoyer tes habits, ils sont sont tâché,*" she said to Gabin one day, pointing him to the sink at the front of the classroom. Then speaking to the class, she said, "*Venir en classe avec des habits tâchés, ce n'est pas respecteux.*"

She turned to Anna with a proud smile. "I say to him that his habits are tasked. It is not respectful to come to class with tasked habits."

"His *clothes* are *stained*," Abeni giggled quietly. "It's not respectful to come to class with *stained clothes*."

Anna smiled, but then stopped when she noticed Gabin sitting back down in his seat behind Chloé. Chloé had her phone hidden behind her purse in her lap, but a little off to the side, and was gesturing at Gabin to look at it. Anna could just make out a picture of Gabin, to which Chloé had added a sort of filter—he looked like a vagabond with ripped clothes and dirt all over his face. She hid the phone again quickly and collapsed into giggles with Victoire. Gabin's face went a little pink.

It looks like she's finding new targets, Anna thought. In fact, Chloé hadn't really bothered her since the incident with Monsieur Beauharnais. She tried, of course—occasionally making ghost sounds over her shoulder—but only between classes and not in front of the teachers anymore. Maybe it was because on the day they got back from Christmas vacation, Chloé had made the mistake of laughing at the way Anna struggled to pronounce a word in French in front of Madame Marel.

"Do you know why we don't make fun of anyone who speaks with an accent?" she said in French, frowning at Chloé. "Because a person speaking with an accent is speaking in a foreign language. That means that they are brave. Brave to learn the language, and brave to speak if they aren't sure that they will be understood."

Anna smiled at her teacher. She was grateful for the defense, and appreciated even more Madame Marel's attempts at speaking English, even though it wasn't perfect.

Anna would even have stopped believing Chloé's ghosts jokes, but when she got home from school that day, an incident occurred in the den that rattled her nerves again. She went there straightaway after school to get some reading done for French class, and to avoid having to stay too long in the living room across the hall, where Rose and her family were saying heartfelt goodbyes to Olivia, thanking her endlessly for the beautiful engagement party and wishing her a good trip to wherever she was going next.

The den would give her some relief—it had a nice view of the back yard that sloped into some vineyards beyond. She opened the door, took a step inside, then froze in her tracks, her heart beating wildly.

The room was in disarray.

Nearly all the books on a bottom shelf had been knocked off and strewn around the floor. Her book for class, which she had placed on the oak coffee table, had also fallen to the ground. Anna ran over to a pile of her own books which were lying topsy-turvy near her cushions and snatched a few up from the floor. Then she looked all around her and saw that luckily, nothing had been damaged. No torn pages, no missing covers. Her breath caught just a little—then she had an idea. A lock wouldn't stop a phantom from entering—if it happened again, she would know why.

I'll ask Mom for a lock for this door. Then I'll know if it's a ghost, once and for all, she thought, her stomach twisting in knots. *And Chloé will finally be off my last nerve.*

CHAPTER 21

A Snobby Rich American Girl

Fleur Castle was seeing constant motion and activity for the rest of winter. Rose dropped by frequently to work on various aspects of the flowers shop and wedding with Mom: designing the set-up of shelves, discussing who would give which speech when and of course, and handmaking some of the decorations. While Anna felt the excitement, she couldn't participate in these activities: she had been getting quite a lot of homework lately, and her little spare time was spent on the Rose dress, which was almost finished. On the weekends, she was often invited over to Abeni's house to work on homework together or watch videos or help her father cook meals inspired from places they had lived before.

There was another reason she avoided participating in the wedding and shop preparation activities. If Rose and Mom weren't discussing Olivia, Rose was opening yet another package containing some type of gift or card from wherever Olivia and her family were in the world at that time. One evening in February, Anna learned that Her Royal Highness was back when Rose gasped and almost yelled "Oh my goodness, it's gorgeous!", her enthusiasm carrying over from the living room into the kitchen.

"I didn't mean diamonds," Rose laughed. "But thanks for finding me a matching bracelet."

"It will pair with your necklace perfectly," Carlotta said excitedly. Anna didn't need to see the bracelet to know that it was magnificent. When Anna went upstairs to her bedroom soon after in a fit of eye-rolling, she began to have doubts about whether her gift could ever compare. She wasn't even sure the dress would even fit Rose properly, since she had no way of knowing how she get Rose's measurements without spoiling the surprise.

She crossed her bedroom to her desk, looking for a book, her phone—anything to distract her—and tripped.

She found herself suddenly face down on the white carpet, not quite realizing for a second what had happened, before turning around to find the culprit.

One sight of it and her mouth dropped open in horror. A dress from the trunk was curled around her left foot, and near the closet, a few were strewn across the floor. Several roses had fallen out of the train of the pink one, and the shiny green one had small tears across the skirt. She looked around desperately for the Rose dress. It was nowhere to be seen.

She snatched up the pink one and another piece of cloth caught her eye: she recognized the shiny red glove that had been lying underneath it. Anger welled up in Anna's chest. It all made sense. Every time Olivia had been to the castle, something strange had happened to Anna's things: a book had gone missing, strange noises were made near the living room window, a dress had been found in another part of the home, a mess had been made in the den and now... this. Her anger grew as she realized how stupid she had been to believe Chloé's silly stories about ghosts. There were no ghosts at Fleur. Only a snobby rich American girl bent on proving how superior she was to Anna.

CHAPTER 22

Anger

Anna stormed into the living room, glaring at Olivia. "Stop touching my stuff!" she yelled.

Olivia, Mom, Rose and Henry stared at her, open-mouthed. No one moved or said a word, so Anna stormed over the Olivia's chair, stood before the girl, and planted her hands firmly on her hips. While before she would have been intimidated by the shine of Olivia's jewelry or perfect shiny hair, Anna's anger seemed to erase all these details as she glared forcefully into the other girl's eyes.

Anna held up the glove. "You were in my room. And my dresses are torn and the Rose one is missing. Give it back!"

Olivia coiled backward, and her eyes shifted to Rose, back to Anna, and then again to Rose, pleading with her cousin to help her find words.

"Anna," Rose said, standing up. "What's wrong?"

Anna whirled around. Her eyes caught on Rose's wrist. She was wearing the gorgeous bracelet. This infuriated Anna even more. What good was a missing handmade dress against Olivia's shining diamonds? Rose had suddenly become very... fancy. She now wanted diamonds and fancy parties, not decorated scraps of cloth and deep, intimate conversation, Anna realized, and now she definitely wanted Rose to know how awful her cousin was. She looked Rose in the eyes, feeling angry, hurt, and desperate.

"Olivia stole a dress I was making! She threw my stuff all over the den. And my sewing! Ruined! All of it!"

"I didn't go to your room," Olivia said, her eyes getting even wider. "I don't even know what the den is. And I don't know what's going on."

"Olivia hasn't been here long," Rose babbled.

"Maybe you put the dress somewhere else?" Mom said. "You were sewing downstairs yesterday."

"Or left it in the den?" Henry said, scrunching up his nose.

Anna threw down the glove and was now shouting. "I found this in my room. She was there! And every time she's come to visit, something gets messed up! From my room! From the den! Why don't you believe me?"

The others just stared back until Mom stood up and walked over to Anna, placing a hand on her shoulder.

"We'll find them," Mom said. "But it wasn't Olivia. She was with Rose ever since she got here and—"

"You always believe her!" Anna exploded, her anger now pouring out of her eyes in tears and her entire body stiffening as if preparing to hit something. "Just because she can play the piano and has thousands of followers and diamond necklaces and..." she took a sharp, deep breath and glared at Henry, then at Olivia. "She's not innocent just because she's rich!"

Olivia turned bright red, and her eyes filled with tears. Anna was almost shocked at the reaction. Olivia always seemed so happy, so enthusiastic, that Anna couldn't imagine her capable of crying. An ounce of sympathy almost welled up in her chest, before dissolving again into anger.

"She's not as great as you all think!"

Then she ran from the room and fled back up the stairs, carried forward by anger but also by shame. She knew she might have been wrong. Mom had presented proof that Olivia was not guilty of stealing, but Anna wanted to believe it so badly. That way, Olivia wouldn't seem so perfect to everyone anymore.

CHAPTER 23

A Field Trip

"Do you want to talk about it?"

Mom was on her way to the city, so she was driving Anna to school the next morning, Anna leaning her right cheek on her seatbelt strap as they sped past fields of melting snow. She answered her mom's question with a shrug of her left shoulder. She didn't particularly want to talk at all, feeling halfway between the anger and shame of the day before, and not knowing how to describe it. She had avoided everyone that evening, throwing herself into her homework in her room, scribbling her way through her math homework, her pen shaking under her hard grip. She didn't want to join them for dinner, and Carlotta didn't press her into it. She had tried to start a conversation when she came back with a plate of soup and a sandwich, but Anna had been too angry to speak.

Her mom didn't press the issue this morning, either, and they drove the rest of the way to school in silence.

"Olivia felt very bad yesterday," Mom said, as they approached the building. "She spent the whole day searching the castle for your dress, even though I told her it wasn't worth it. She found it, by the way. She wants to give it to you herself."

Anna was relieved, but stilled played mute.

"She's a very nice girl," Carlotta continued. "She may live in a different world from us, but she's kind and has always wanted so badly to be your friend. Did you know she got mad at Henry because he didn't invite you to that Matthis's party? Not that I would have let you anyway, but it was thoughtful of her."

Anna swallowed, feeling even more guilty but not wanting to give up her anger towards Olivia.

"And we don't care if she's rich or has a big house or lots of followers," Mom sighed. "Her life is not as easy as it looks, you know. Everyone has struggles in their lives, no matter how perfect they look."

"But she stole my dress," Anna said, then undid her seatbelt, and got out of the car. She was tired of adults always siding with people who annoyed her— first Chloé in Monsieur Beauharnais's class, now Olivia with her family. She waved goodbye to her mom, who sighed and smiled sadly after her. Anna felt a second of regret for making Carlotta sad, but forgot it as Abeni ran up to her in the courtyard.

"We don't have to go upstairs first," her friend said. "The bus is already here!"

Anna suddenly remembered that the class was going on a field trip today, one that Anna had been looking forward to. Monsieur Beauharnais was bringing them to a World War II museum in the city.

After looking around and confirming that Olivia wouldn't be joining them today, she smiled at Abeni and pointed to her light spring jacket, then put out her foot to show her white sneakers which she wore with blue jeans. Abeni had decided she wanted to wear matching colors with Anna every day, and Anna, taking this as a sign that Abeni was her best friend after the doll incident and every other doubt she had had before, was happy to go along with it. She was glad it was still cool outside and that she didn't have to wear a crop-top for now.

The bus ride wasn't long, and when they stepped off, Anna was glad to see two flags in front of the museum, one French and one American. Monsieur Beauharnais and the tour guide—a portly man with little glasses and a balding head—led them through room after room of pictures of soldiers. They explained that some were American and some French, but that they had all fought together against the Germans who had invaded France during World War II. While

Monsieur Beauharnais looked like he was trying not to roll his eyes, Abeni beamed proudly at Anna a few times, and at the end, the tour guide looked right at her when he explained that he was personally grateful to her country. His grandfather had survived the war only because an American soldier had found him wounded and saved his life when he got trapped under rubble.

"I would not be here today if not for the Americans," he said in English to Anna. Her classmates smiled excitedly, except Chloé, of course, who pretended she hadn't heard and continued her whispered conversation with Victoria.

They ended the day at the large gift shop full of American-themed jewelry, keychains, and clothes. Anna was delighted and was also happy to look through some books and their black-and-white pictures of French and American soldiers working and celebrating together on battlefields, boats and rubble. As she and Abeni poured over the books, Anna's eyes caught some strange movements at the center of the shop.

Chloé seemed to be having convulsions, jerking her head and hands around and rolling her eyes back in her head. Victoria, however, was shaking with silent laughter at her side, so Anna wasn't worried, and Chloé, too, collapsed into giggles when she was done, like she did when she was doing ghost impressions. Anna turned her back to the two; and then, on the other end of the store, she saw a familiar face.

Olivia was standing at the checkout counter behind an elegantly-dressed woman, whose back was to Chloé. The woman's sleek dark hair matched Olivia's, and something in her demeanor, too. Olivia was staring straight at Chloé, her face completely red. A man was next to Olivia, facing her at an angle so that he couldn't see Chloé, and was holding Olivia's hand. The two adults were clearly her parents. Anna looked back at Chloé, open-mouthed, for she had just understood who Chloé was making fun of. Olivia's father was in a wheelchair, hunched over, with thin legs and trembling hands. Every so often, his head jerked lightly to the side in an uncontrolled motion.

Then Anna saw Olivia's eyes well up with angry tears, much in the same way they had when Anna had accused her of stealing of her dress. Her mother and father hadn't noticed Chloé, and were heading towards the exit, her mother's hand on the father's as he rolled along in his chair. Olivia followed, throwing one last glance at Anna, a fearful look in her eyes. At that moment, Anna realized that her mom had been right about Olivia. Olivia was in the exact same position that Anna had been in when she had had to face Lilith at her old school. Everything made sense now.

Everyone has struggles in their lives, no matter how perfect they look.

Anna had been angry when she confronted Olivia about the Rose dress, but her anger had been about jealousy over unimportant things, like money and fame. Now her anger was in the name of justice—justice for Olivia against Chloé, justice for herself against Lilith, justice for anyone who had been bullied, but also justice for Olivia against the false accusations Anna had made against her with no real proof. This anger was better, more purposeful, and it gave her courage. Anna gave her bag to Abeni, and marched over to Chloé, her fists clenched and ready, a little American soldier ready for battle on French soil.

CHAPTER 24

Battle

"*Ce n'est pas drôle,*" Anna said loudly, planting herself in front of Chloé. "Not funny!"

The entire store went quiet. Even the noise of the forty students crammed into the area slowly died away. Anna continued in French without even realizing it.

"It's very stupid to make fun of someone like that! He never did anything to you, and Olivia either! She is ten times what you are! She dresses better and is world-famous! Is that why you're mocking her dad? Because you know she is better than you and you're trying to make her feel bad. But she won't. Olivia is a queen. She's talented, and kind, and pretty, and..."

She looked at the door. Olivia's parents were well beyond the threshold, but Olivia had stopped. Her back was still turned towards Anna, but her chest

143

was obviously heaving. Then Anna looked around and noticed all the eyes on her. She felt that familiar tightening of her stomach when too many people were watching her, but when she looked back at Olivia once more, her anger at Chloé kept her going.

"Stop making fun of people, Chloé," Anna said, still loudly but more calmly, and this time in English. "Stop making fun of me, or Olivia, or Gabin, or anyone else you feel inferior to. If you think someone is better than you, work harder on yourself. Or just be confident in who you are and stop comparing yourself to others! But stop trying to tear them down. Abeni will translate."

Abeni didn't need to do anything. Chloé had understood the message, even if she hadn't understood the words. She looked from Anna to those around her, unsure of what to do. She couldn't seem to tell if everyone was shocked at Anna's anger, or on her side. Victoria looked equally confused. Then Gabin spoke up.

"*Anna a raison,*" he said. "*Tu te moques des autres pour les rebaisser parce que tu n'as pas confiance en toi-même.*"

Now it was Anna's turn to be surprised. Not only had Gabin spoken up, but he had said something intelligent: "You make fun of others to bring them down because you don't have confidence in yourself."

Suddenly, Anna noticed that Delphine was nodding in agreement. Several other students were, too.

"Yeah, stop those dumb posts about me," Delphine said. "I don't actually think they're funny."

Something in Anna relaxed.

Chloé, however, turned bright red.

"You have wrong," Chloé said to Anna. "Not jealous. You? No, not jealous of you or Olivia or Gabin. Victoria, *on y va*." And Victoria followed her out of the store but glanced back uneasily at the crowd. Anna had noticed in the way Chloé answered that she had spoken differently than she usually did, as if she were nervous, and had even blushed very faintly, something she had never done before. Anna watched them go and brush past Olivia, who was still frozen near the doorway.

The hubbub in the store rose again, and Anna made her way back to the shelf she had been looking at before. She passed her classmates, some of whom carried on as if nothing had happened, but she noticed some of them throwing her shy, proud smiles, including Delphine, who burst into giggles as she watched Chloé and Victoria storm away. Anna felt reassured that she had done the right thing, but Olivia had left. Maybe she hadn't appreciated what Anna had done—after all, it had exposed the fact that someone was mocking her father. Maybe she would never have a chance to make up with Olivia after all.

"Anna," Abeni whispered when Anna got back to her. "Good job! You got angry in French!"

Anna looked at her, puzzled.

"My dad says that when someone can feel big emotions and express them in a foreign language, they truly speak the language," Abeni explained.

Anna beamed with pride. She didn't need to be jealous of anyone when she had her own skill: perfect, angry French.

CHAPTER 25

A New Friend

When Anna entered the living room that evening, Rose was sitting near the fireplace, an open book in her lap, a glass of iced tea in her hands and Pamplemousse at her feet. She had been staring silently into the empty hearth when Anna arrived. It seemed as if she had been awaiting her arrival. She turned towards the girl and smiled sadly.

"Would you like to have some with me?" she asked and nodded to a little jug filled with iced tea. Another cup was waiting on a white tray, as well as a jug full of lemonade.

Anna opted for the lemonade, its sweet smell untying the knots that had formed in her stomach when she had seen Rose. As Rose filled a glass, Anna noticed that she wasn't wearing diamonds anymore.

Not knowing what to say, Anna blurted out, "Where's your bracelet?"

Rose looked at her quizzically. "Bracelet? I never wear bracelets."

"The one Olivia gave you."

Rose sighed and smiled. "I'll only wear that for my wedding. It's not really my style, you know. I just wore it yesterday to please Olivia. She really likes to do nice things for people."

She looked at Anna meaningfully and held out the glass

Anna clasped her hands around it, but she didn't drink yet. She was too anxious about what Rose would say about the night Anna had yelled at Olivia.

"Olivia told me what happened at the museum today," Rose said. "That was a good thing you did, especially after all Chloé has done to you." She paused. "Olivia told me about that."

Anna was taken aback, half glad that Rose had chosen the positive incident to start, half embarrassed that she had purposely glossed over the ugly one. Anna sank into the chair slowly so as not to upset her glass, and tentatively took a sip, still unsure of what to say. A few more sips helped her find her voice.

"I didn't know about her dad," Anna said. "Maybe I would have been nicer. But I was so mad because, well, she has so much money and buys you nice gifts and...

and... I felt like you had forgotten me when she got here... and..."

"Anna," Rose interrupted, smiling kindly. "How could I forget you? I've just been so busy preparing the wedding and my shop. There's so much to do and whenever Olivia and her family offered to help, I was so in over my head that I couldn't say no. Besides, they always seemed to want to pay me back for when I took care of Olivia. It seemed to make them happy. I didn't realize that you felt slighted."

"Took care of Olivia?"

"Sort of," Rose said. "Her father got very sick many years ago. Luckily, he and his wife had amassed a fortune, so financially they'll always be ok, but it really hurt Olivia. I think she blames herself for him getting sick, which is strange because she had nothing to do with it. Isn't it strange how people feel guilty for things that they didn't do? Maybe it's their way of explaining the inexplicable to themselves."

Anna understood. Lillith and Chloé had always made her feel like the bullying was her own fault: if only she had worn the right clothes, had the right hobbies...

"She's been trying really hard to please her father," Rose continued. "Many kids with her money would just waste it on silly things but she's tried to succeed in school, the piano, and everything she thinks will make her dad happy. She puts so much pressure on herself..." Rose trailed off with a sigh, then continued: "I moved in after the accident to sort of, keep her occupied and give her some company while her parents were away for treatments. She was too young to have to deal with all that. Not like a nanny—God knows they had enough of those—but to be there for her, go to her concerts when her mother was too sad to go..." Her voice faded away again, then returned.

"Olivia's mother was very attached to the idea that her daughter never become spoiled and that she live a normal life beyond the luxuries at home." Rose finally smiled. "Of course, they could never be completely normal, but they don't look down on others, and despite my uncle's accident, they've been very generous to many charitable causes."

Anna nodded and placed her glass on the coffee table.

"Pretty dresses and fame can't make everything better, I guess," Anna said, leaning forward to place her elbows on her knees and cupping her head in her hands.

Rose smiled. "Exactly. But I'm glad she has it. She works hard on her piano and does it out of love. She—"

Rose was interrupted by Pamplemousse's plump body suddenly landing in her lap. He had jumped from the mantle onto the chair, upsetting a stack of books that had been shelved over the fireplace and leaving puffs of orange fur in his wake. The books tumbled sideways and slid behind a floor cabinet that stood next to the fireplace. The round feline stared at them, then pounced on a red leather-bound volume, gently gnawing a corner. Rose gasped.

"Pamplemousse! Be careful! You're making a mess."

Seeming not to hear, he batted a small book of poetry. It too fell to the floor from atop its pile. Then he took it in his mouth, meowed softly and jumped onto Rose's lap.

"He always plays with books," Rose laughed, stroking his head. "I thinks he's jealous of them because I read them so much! He wants me to give him attention, too! And what's this?"

Rose gently pulled on a piece of green cloth that seemed to have gotten stuck in his collar. Pamplemousse simply yawned and curled up on Rose's lap in the shape of an oversize shrimp. His eyes closed immediately, and he began to purr.

Anna watched the spectacle, then suddenly her mouth flew open as Rose uncrumpled the bit of cloth. It was a green bodice from one of the doll dresses.

"The books!" she exclaimed. "And my dresses! It was Pamplemousse!"

She jumped up and clasped a hand to her forehead.

"It all makes sense!" she said. "Every time you were at the castle, something happened to my stuff! But it wasn't because you were with Olivia, it's because Pamplemousse follows you everywhere!"

"I guess you won't be coming here anymore," Rose said, wagging her finger at the orange cat who blinked at her gently as if he hadn't a care in the world, then laid down his head again for a snooze.

Anna took the cloth Rose was holding out to her and went up to her room. She found the dress in question and was relieved to see that Pamplemousse had detached the whole piece and not torn anything. Then, a knock startled her.

Olivia was standing at the door. She clasped her hands in front of her and looked at Anna with a gentle smile. But something had changed. It took Anna a minute to realize that her eyes were pleading, and she wasn't carrying her shoulders in that usual, confident position. She was wearing nothing but a plain white dress. No fancy hat or ribbons, no rings. It seemed so... *off*, Anna thought. Olivia was not herself without her usual attire.

The girls stared at each other for a second. Anna wasn't sure if Olivia had heard her when she had solved the mystery of the missing books.

"I'm sorry," they both blurted out at the same time.

"Why are *you* sorry?" they both said.

They stopped, then both began to giggle.

"Ok, me first," Olivia said. "I'm sorry if I made you feel bad. I'm sorry that I did too much for Rose. I had no idea you admired her so much."

Anna shook her head. "I'm sorrier. I've only known Rose for a short time and you're practically sisters. And

I didn't take the time to understand you. I judged you by your dresses instead of your personality."

Olivia shrugged. "I should have understood not to show off my fashion here, but I thought the French were super-fashionable and I was afraid of not fitting in."

"Like crop-tops," Anna mumbled.

"What's that?" Olivia asked.

"Everyone wears crop-tops at school, but I hate them," Anna said. "But I want to fit in here and Abeni wears them too..."

"Yeah, peer pressure is so annoying," Olivia said. "I guess sometimes social media gets to me, too, and I compare myself to other people. They always post their best outfits, all the trendy places they go and always look so happy... well, I guess I can have a jealous streak sometimes."

Anna was startled to think that Olivia, too, could feel inferior to others, even from her position in life.

"Well, that's the problem when you have struggles, I guess," Olivia added, as if reading Anna's thoughts. "You only see the perfection in others and forget that they can have problems, too."

Anna nodded.

"Yeah, this year, moving to France and all, I've mostly just felt... anxious and exasperated and, well, unhappy..." Anna said. "And since you looked perfect and talented and happy all the time... "

She sighed.

"I'm sorry about the piano," Olivia said sadly. "Maybe I *was* showing off a little, but I really wanted you guys to like me. And the piano doesn't necessarily make me happy. It's hard to explain. But I am at peace and content when I play. My dad always says that being content with what we have and at peace with what's around us is more important than being happy." She frowned, as if thinking deeply about those words. Anna did the same.

"But I won't show off so much on the piano anymore. And I'm going to get rid of the dresses and purses and shoes, at least while I'm living here. I have too many!"

Anna stood up. "No!" she exclaimed. "Olivia, those clothes are beautiful. And the piano. They're *you* and they make you... royal!"

"Are you sure?" Olivia asked.

"I love the clothes," Anna said. "You look like royalty walking around this... French château. We need Rose's wedding to be classy, and her opening day, too. Maybe you can teach me how to dress."

Anna glanced down at her crop top hidden under a cardigan.

"I tried to fit in too, but this stuff just isn't me," she sighed.

"Let's change for dinner," Olivia said. "I could lend you a dress tonight and show you how to pair accessories, if you let me borrow those pretty flower earrings you're wearing."

Anna touched her ears and widened her eyes.

"Mom got these for just a few euros at a street vendor," she laughed.

"I don't care," Olivia said. "They're so pretty. And you know, I don't get all my clothes in expensive stores. The fur we found in Sweden was at a street market... I may have made it sound fancier than it is. Again, wanting everyone to like me... and a tad worried that when everyone saw your amazing dresses, they would think mine were lame."

"Really?" Anna laughed and started taking out her earrings.

"Rose told me about them," Olivia said. "You really should start your own Instagram. I bet you could sell them!"

If Rose had mentioned Anna's dresses, she really had liked them. This, in addition to Olivia's admiration, thrilled Anna.

"We actually have a lot in common," Anna sighed, handing over her earrings.

"Pretty dresses," Olivia said.

"Flowers," Anna added.

"Trying to fit in."

"Comparing ourselves too much with others."

The girls looked at each other and laughed.

"Let's not do that anymore," Anna said.

"Yeah. Just wear what we want and be who we are."

"And be content with what we have."

"And at peace with what's around us," they said at the same time, and then laughed.

"Deal," Anna held out her hand. "We could have been good friends. I hope it's not too late."

"No, it's not," Olivia laughed, pulling out her own earrings to replace them with the flowers. "We certainly got off on the wrong foot."

"Friends, then," Anna grinned.

"Not just friends!" Olivia exclaimed. "Do you want to be a Junior Bridesmaid, too?"

"Do you think Rose will mind?" Anna asked.

"I already asked her!" Olivia said. "Of course she said yes. Do you have time to make two more dresses?"

"Yes!" Anna grinned, not bothering to actually calculate the time that was left before the wedding. "We're going to be the most beautiful Flower Girls this castle has ever seen!"

"But there's something else we have to do first," Olivia said. "Rose's shop is opening in just three weeks!"

CHAPTER 26

Back to Royalty

"What are we wearing today?" Abeni's frantic voice was on the phone at 7am on a Saturday. Anna rolled over sleepily.

"Uh... Rose said casual because we have to move around a lot," Anna answered.

"Ok, white sneakers, jeans and crop?"

"Uh..." Anna sat up. She didn't want to hurt her friend's feelings. "Ok. The black one?"

"Alright," Abeni agreed. "Be at the gate in 10."

Then Anna glanced in the corner of her room where two half-finished junior bridesmaid's dresses were draped over their mannequins, pins of all colors stuck all up and down the sides. The flowing skirts reminded Anna of springtime... and royalty, of course.

She sighed. She didn't want a crop top. She wanted her own style.

She put on the jeans and sneakers but replaced the crop top with a regular black shirt.

"Oh, I thought I heard 'crop'," Abeni said when Anna opened the gate.

"Um, to be honest…" Anna sighed. "I don't really like crop tops."

"So why wear them?" Abeni shrugged, looking puzzled.

Anna was so relieved.

"I guess I just… want to fit in," she said.

"Pssshhh what's Nella's number one rule?" Abeni asked, planting her hands on her hips.

"Wear what only you can rock," Anna sang.

"And we still match anyway," Abeni grinned. They hooked arms and made their way to the village center.

It seemed as if everyone who lived in town and a few square miles around was present for the Grand Opening. It seemed as if flowers had become the most sought-after commodity in the area. And it seemed as if springtime had arrived just in time to add extra sunshine to the day.

"Thanks for the extra volunteer," Rose whispered to Anna, looking at Abeni. "And we need more macarons, please."

Anna and Abeni rushed to the back to look for more platters.

"Already?" Olivia said, pulling open another box of the colorful cookies and spreading them on to a tray.

"They're going almost as fast as the flowers," Anna said. "Jean-Luc is good."

The flowers were indeed disappearing quickly, too. Even though Rose and Alex had stocked the floor-to-ceiling shelves, and several racks outside, Anna wondered if they would last the day. She returned to the front counter with Abeni and the tray.

It was busy and almost frantic out front, but Anna was glad—Rose had been anxious about drawing in enough customers on the first day, and the hubbub in the store was proof that she had.

"Mom said she'll come back tomorrow for more," Delphine said, plopping a pile of roses on the counter just as Anna got back.

"*Et ces guirlandes, vous les vendez?*" an older woman behind Delphine inquired. "*Les fleurs sont magnifiques !*"

"She said—" Delphine began.

"I know," Anna said, proud that her French was now good enough to gotten all of what the woman had said, and prouder still of *what* had been said: "And are you selling those garlands? The flowers are beautiful!"

"*Non,*" Anna replied. "*C'est juste de la déco.*"

"Just decoration for now," Olivia said, from the doorway of the back room. "But Anna will start her own business someday. Felt flowers that look completely real."

The two shared a smile.

And before she knew it, Anna was watching her good friend Rose get married. It was a magnificent affair, Anna thought—but not just because of the masses of flowers that decked out the garden at Fleur, nor horse-drawn carriage and other elegant touches that Olivia's family had added. Rose wore a huge smile on her face as she practically skipped down the aisle, swinging her new husband's hand under a shower of petals from the guests.

"Hey, our turn!" Olivia whispered, nudging Anna. They were both standing on chairs near the end of the aisle, wearing matching light pink dresses with flowing, silky skirts and a flowered belt at the waist.

"Oh, right," Anna said, remembering that she had a whole basket of petals that needed to be thrown at the very end. She held it up as high as she could and overturned the contents on the happy couple who laughed and turned to each other for one last kiss, to the delight of the photographer at their feet and loud cheers from the guests.

Next it was time for the traditional *apéro*. They knew a full meal was coming after, but the guests didn't hold back on filling their plates with finger food and sipping down a few drinks. When Henry discovered that more food was being stored in the kitchen, he stole away a few times to bring back heaping plates to Anna, Olivia, and Abeni while Carlotta rolled her eyes.

"Someday, Henry, I'll teach you what the French call *'la délicatesse'*"", she said with a sigh, shooing the children towards the fountain to take pictures with the bride and groom.

The bride was weaving her way through the guests to greet them and when she saw Anna, she gave her a hug.

"I love it," she said, gesturing to the gift table near the door of the château where the dinner would be held later. "Exquisite. Thank you, My Little American!"

In the middle of the table was a glass case, and inside, the Rose dress— perfectly tailored to Rose's size thanks to information that Olivia had gathered when she went dress shopping with Rose and then passed along to Anna. Anna had finished it just hours before the ceremony.

Rose was gone before Anna could reply, off to hug and kiss the other ninety guests, starting with Olivia's parents, who were in deep conversation with Anna's.

After dinner, the guests were brought outside and stood behind the bride and groom as the most beautiful fireworks Anna had ever seen exploded above the castle, illuminating the entire building and the grounds beyond.

Olivia winced and looked sheepishly at Anna.

"I knew how much Rose wanted fireworks," she said. "I couldn't resist asking my mom..."

"It's ok," Anna grinned. "They're magnificent. Rose is so excited! And your father looks so happy, too!"

Olivia put her arm around Anna's shoulder and Anna put hers around Olivia's waist. As the gentle classical music that had accompanied the fireworks broke into thudding dance music, the girls broke ranks and joined the guests on the dance floor.

And Anna decided she was content here as she glanced happily around at her mom, her dad, Henry, Abeni, and Olivia. The same feeling of peace that she had felt last summer before all the drama of the school year had returned. After all, Château Fleur had once again become a place of wonder where Anna could live in royal comfort—not because of its grand antique rooms or magnificent gardens, but because it was a place of friendships, new and old.

Acknowledgements

would like to thank all my readers for their support, especially those who offer encouragement and feedback. I am also grateful to my children for the inspiration they provide, simply by being the beautiful souls they are. Finally, a heartfelt thank you to my husband for supporting everything I do and believing in everything I create.